The Underwater Detectives

Catherine Copeland
Artwork by Marjolein Scott-van der Hek

Lily Publications

First published 2009

Lily Publications Ltd, PO Box 33, Ramsey, Isle of Man IM99 4LP

ISBN 978-1-899602-45-2

Typeset in ITC Usherwood

The Red Cap

"Responsible residents of the Isle of Man say that they have seen mermaids — some with red hair — in recent years. The colour of the hair recalls the enchanted red cap of legendary Irish mermaids …"

— Gwen Benwell and Arthur Waugh, *Sea Enchantress*

It was Saturday morning and Merryn was in the kitchen doing her usual Saturday morning stuff. As she fed some suspicious looking green sludge into a sausage-making machine, Mum sealed off each of the emerging sausages with a small ball-bearing followed by a pin, before carefully stacking them into a wooden crate labelled 'grenades'.

Dad was leaning over the stove stirring a large pot of boiling water. Merryn watched out of the corner of her eye as he added to it a bottle of black dye followed by a bottle of purple dye. He stirred the pot again before plopping into the dark brew a pair of jeans, a shirt made out of some stretchy material, two mismatched socks and some underpants. Blurple was Dad's favourite colour.

The doorbell rang and she jumped.

"I'll get it."

Rushing to rinse the green stuff from her hands she felt a surge of panic. *What if it's Susie Cooil or the Ellison twins?* Merryn never mentioned her family to friends and never, ever invited them to her house after school or at weekends. Anyway, she much preferred to visit one of their houses. No dad strutting around in fancy dress from thirty years ago and no munitions factory in the kitchen.

Tearing down the hallway she held her breath and opened up. *Phew!* It was local police constable Quirk.

"Hello, Merryn isn't it? Is your mum at home?" The PC took off his hat and stepped inside.

I wonder why he's here ... Merryn led him to the kitchen where Mum was now working on a massive project that took up the whole of the dining room table. It resembled a giant Christmas pudding and was referred to as the WMD. The weapon of mass destruction consisted of a huge bomb that, once detonated, could deploy a ten-second spray of fluorescent green paint at a blast radius of twenty feet. As Mum spotted the visitor she downed tools and stood up.

Mum and PC Quirk had gone to school together. They were old friends.

"Hey, Quirky! What's up? Word travels quick round here. Not breaking any laws building this thing, am I?"

"Probably, but that's not why I'm here. I'm afraid I have

some bad news Sharon. Maybe you should sit back down?"

Mum put an arm around Merryn but remained standing. Merryn decided it must be okay for her to stay.

Quirk paused and looked down at the floor. As Dad turned from the stove to listen, Merryn felt an icy sensation crawl down the length of her body. This didn't feel too good.

Quirk took a deep breath and looked up again. "Lorelei's dead."

Auntie ... Great-Aunt Lorelei ... Merryn felt her mind go blank for a couple of seconds before the shock slammed into it. Just as she felt her knees begin to buckle a second shock hit her. She saw Mum's hands fly up to her face as if in slow motion. For a moment she looked like she was going to scream then suddenly she was composed again. Mum led an army into paintball battle every weekend. She was the toughest person Merryn knew.

Mum squeezed her shoulder then sat back down, pulling her close.

"Did she go quietly, in her sleep?" Mum asked.

"I'm afraid not. She was found early this morning by Benny Quill while he was walking his dog. She'd been washed up on the beach at Ben-Varrey Bay. I don't think her passing is suspicious. She is ... was ... elderly."

"She swims from Ben-Varrey Bay to Sea Lion Cove every morning."

"I know. It's a strenuous swim, but still, I'm a bit surprised. I spoke to her just two days ago, down in the village. She was in good nick, your aunt. We'll have the coroner investigate but as I say, nothing seems suspicious at this stage. I'm sorry to have to be the one to tell you. She was a remarkable lady."

Quirk was interrupted by the shrill ring of the telephone.

"Reporters, I expect. I'll leave you to it. You know where to find me."

As Dad accompanied Quirk to the door, Mum picked up the phone. Merryn gazed out of the back window. She stared across to the calm waters at the rear of the property. Her chest hurt. She folded her arms across it, hugging herself.

Mum's loud and perfectly controlled telephone voice filtered through. *At least she seems normal again.*

"… Lorelei Moore was special to all of us. A handsome woman and one of the best swimmers this island ever produced. She never missed her daily swim and I believe she still holds the record for being the first woman to swim the Minch … What's that? The Minch? The Minch is that spooky passage of water — a bit like the Bermuda Triangle. It's off the coast of Scotland. Countless boats and fishermen have disappeared in the Minch, some on the calmest of days. Auntie used to say that the ghosts of dead fishermen, lured to their deaths by mermen — or 'merrow' as she always called them — haunted this stretch. It took courage to swim it, and there was a rumour, put about by the one boat brave enough to follow her, that she somehow achieved most of it underwater! She was a great character and a credit to the island. We'll miss her enormously …"

Shortly after the policeman's visit, the household was interrupted by yet another ring. This time it was the door again. Merryn flew along the hallway and wrenched it open. She inhaled deeply, the breath clinging to the back of her throat. *Please, let it be a mistake.* The breath gushed back out. It was the postman. In his hand was a brown paper parcel secured with string and addressed to her.

She signed for the package, then closed the door and carried it through to the kitchen. Staring down at the sender's name, the heavy feeling increased in the pit of her stomach — like she was about to hurtle down a white-knuckle ride. She stopped in the kitchen doorway and stared. Her older brothers Declan and Dave were home from football practice and the family was in the kitchen preparing for lunch. *How can they be so normal? They'll never see her again.*

"Who's knockin'?" inquired Dad. "Reporters again, no doubt. Invited 'em in, I hope?"

He whipped out a comb and gazed at his reflection in the gleaming oven door. Then he slipped the comb back into his pocket.

"Can't improve upon perfection."

Merryn interrupted Declan's sniggers. "It was the postman ... for me. It's a parcel. I ... it's from Aunt Lorelei!"

The family stopped what they were doing and stared at the box.

"She must have posted it yesterday ... before her swim," stammered Merryn. "Her last swim ..."

"Well, open it!" said Mum. For once, her voice was on the quiet side.

Hands shaking, Merryn ripped off the outer wrapping and tore open the box flaps to reveal a single item; a small red cap. It was plain and dome-shaped without a brim or a peak, and appeared to be made from waterproof material decorated with fabric petals. It reminded her of a bathing hat, the type older ladies often wore at the local pool.

"It's Auntie's old swimming cap!" exclaimed Mum. "Haven't seen it in years, not since I was a girl. It's the one she swam the Minch in. She must have wanted you to have it. Strange coincidence she posted it just before … ooh … you don't think …?"

"You mean she topped herself," said Declan.

"Or knew she was about to be bumped off," added Dave.

"Calm down lads," said Dad. "You know how old ladies are. They can sense these things. Take yer great-granny for instance. Before she died, she spent the entire week cooking and freezing bags of food. Deep down, she couldn't bear the thought of Thomas going hungry."

"I thought Great-Granddad's name was Alf," said Declan.

"It was. Thomas was the cat."

"Merryn saw Aunt Lorelei a couple of days ago and she was fine," announced Mum sharply. "She would have said if anything had seemed amiss, wouldn't you, sweetie? So I'll hear no more on the subject until we've heard back from the people who DO know what they're talking about, Declan and David O'Reilly. Your great-aunt's just died and your sister's human even if you're not. Show some respect."

The heaviness deepened. Merryn felt sick. Her thoughts flew back a couple of days to Thursday, after school, the last time she'd seen Auntie alive. They'd been in the kitchen making afternoon tea. She closed her eyes seeing Auntie's strong face, her tanned cheeks framed with thick white hair, still long and wavy like her own. But she'd looked different that day. The tanned cheeks had been pale and she'd put sugar in Merryn's tea. Merryn never had sugar and Aunt Lorelei was never forgetful.

Later, Merryn woke from a deep sleep. She glanced at the clock. It was twelve minutes past midnight and the light from a bright moon flooded through the window, streaming onto her face. Reaching over from her bedside to close the curtains, she noticed the box containing the red cap. In the light of the moon, a crimson glow seemed to be radiating from within. Tentatively, she grasped the box and opened it. Wiping sleep from her eyes, she shook her head. Could this be the same cap she'd seen earlier in the day? Her hands trembled as she picked it up and turned it over.

She saw clearly now that the domed section, which she'd taken to be made of rubber, was actually woven or meshed together with a fine, shimmering silk-like substance. The crimson petals, attached to the outside of the cap, looked more like scales. She stroked them gently, feeling their softness. Peering closer, in the faint light, she saw the truth. Nestled amongst the silk mesh were hundreds of tiny overlapping feathers. Red feathers, like the scarlet plumage of a parrot.

She glimpsed her dark reflection in the windowpane. Tugging gently, she pulled the cap over her head. The mesh seemed to move and contract until it found a snug fit. It was warm and light and she never wanted to take it off. Gazing out across the dark horizon, a strange sensation came over her. In the distance, she could see the sea stretched out like a sheet of grey satin. It was a chilly November night but somehow the sea seemed so inviting. She longed to run across the headland and dive into the cool water … to feel it on her skin … through her hair …

A sudden shaft of light broke the spell. Mum was at the door.

"Time for sleep, love. It's been a long day."

Mum's eyes looked a bit red. Merryn slipped the cap from her head and crawled under the covers, clutching it tightly behind her.

Mum's footsteps disappeared and Merryn opened her bedside drawer. She picked up the torch she had hidden away for reading under the covers. She'd spied something whilst removing the cap. It was a label with some tiny print on it — probably care instructions. Directing the torchlight onto the tag she read the following:

Keep this red cap by your side,
With others it must never bide.
Find its use this precious prize,
It only sparkles for the wise.

She was reading the verse for a second time when a strong hand yanked the bedclothes back. Mum took the cap from her and placed it back in its box. She put the box out of reach and pulled the curtains together.

"Sleep. Now. Do."

Merryn sat alone near the entrance to the canteen. It was the day after Aunt Lorelei's funeral and she was back at school. Someone opened a door and cold air washed over her. She shivered but didn't bother moving. She felt cold anyway.

Putting her barely touched sandwich back in its box, she stole a quick glance at the boy sitting nearby. In that brief moment he looked up and their eyes met. His were dark and liquid-like, fringed with long black lashes. His hair was so fair it gave off a strange silvery sheen. *I haven't seen him before. He must be new.*

As the bell rang and she packed her lunch box into her bag, the boy spoke to her. Her head jolted up. His voice was surprisingly deep yet soft at the same time. It was a nice combination.

"Who do you have this afternoon?" he asked.

"Cretin followed by Kermit. What about you?"

The boy pulled a piece of paper from his pocket and consulted it. Slowly, he began to smile. "The same ... I guess."

She stared at his teeth. They were white and nearly perfect, apart from the eye teeth. These were slightly longer than normal and a bit pointier.

Merryn made her way to the gym alone. She didn't see the boy again until the class had changed and assembled in the main hall. Today was the first indoor PE class of the term.

"Okay troops, shoes and socks off," ordered Mr Crebbin in a voice Mum would have been proud of. "And maybe you can leave your tongue in your shoe today Miss Ellison."

The twin stopped chatting and did as she was told.

"You suffering from non-compliance Rohan Kelly or are you just hard of hearing?"

The boy from the canteen didn't move. A crimson flush spread across his cheeks. Merryn felt her own cheeks redden.

"Well, what are you waiting for?"

The whole class was watching now. Mr Crebbin swaggered across the room. His mean eyes narrowed and his voice dropped to a dangerous quiet.

"You trying to be clever, Kelly?"

"No sir."

"You're new here, so for your benefit I'll tell you what I don't like. I don't like smart Alecs! Remove your socks or maybe I can have them removed for you."

"I ... I've got some verrucas." Rohan looked up meeting the teacher's glare. A couple of the braver students sniggered.

"Show me."

"N ... now?"

Merryn looked down at the floor.

"No Kelly, in Constantinople next year! Second thoughts, you know what? I really don't want to see your foot warts. Wear your socks today and make sure you have a doctor's note next time or you can share your stinkin' feet with the whole class. UNDERSTOOD?"

The lesson passed and Merryn changed back into uniform. She continued on to her final lesson and taking a seat near the back of the room she pulled out her favourite book, *A History of the Sea*. It had been a recent birthday present from Aunt Lorelei. She opened the front cover and traced the inscription with a finger tip.

> *To Merryn,*
> *Our beautiful world holds many mysteries but none so many as the sea. Happy eleven.*
> *Much love, Auntie.*

Mr Kermeen's loud cough broke her concentration. She looked up at the barrel-shaped man and listened as his strange throaty voice cut through the background chatter.

"Afternoon year seven English. Today, during quiet reading, I have an especially rare treat."

She groaned inwardly. He repeated this same line every week.

"Let's sit back, get comfortable, and relax and read to the stirring sounds of Rimsky Korsakov's *Arabian Nights*."

"Excuse me sir." It was Tom Hafey. He held his pen aloft and looked earnest. "Did you say rip yer corsets off?"

Laughter and the sound of palms slapping exploded around the room. Mr Kermeen had to clear his throat several times before reading — quiet reading — could commence.

Later, as the bell sounded and Merryn closed her book preparing to leave, she heard one of Hafey's cronies.

"Whatcha readin' Huff?"

"*Varney the Vampyre.*"

"Kelly looks like a vampire," sneered the crony, Huff's mate, Francis Bourke.

Merryn looked up sharply. Rohan was seated close by.

"Nice one Berk! Verruca Varney, eh?" smirked Huff loudly enough for all to hear. His voice took on a more sinister tone. Merryn shivered.

"Vampires need to know their place."

She sank into the moonlight

Ben-Varrey Bay

"She sank into the moonlight
And the sea was only sea."
 — James Elroy Flecker, *A Legend of the Aegean*

Merryn dreamt about the red cap. She was swimming in warm, pale-green water. A shaft of sunlight penetrated the depths dazzling her. She squinted, her eyes closed tight then opened. She rolled over and gazed upward connecting with the box her mother had placed out of reach some nights before. The sun slipped out from behind clouds and light flooded into the bedroom. She focused. Today was Saturday. She had the whole weekend to try and discover why Aunt Lorelei would send her an old swimming cap.

Could it be sheer coincidence that Auntie's death had timed with her decision to pass on the cap? She dismissed the idea.

Auntie would have given it to her in person, not send it through the post. And then there was the strange verse. The first section of it was straightforward enough. She would never willingly give or lend the cap to anyone, not now it was hers. The final passage was more curious. The cap must have a purpose.

A swimming cap ... too obvious ... feathers ... birds ... flying! She decided to take a walk along the coastal path first thing. Birds nested alongside the cliff and watching them might give her some ideas.

She slipped into corduroy jeans and a thick Arran jumper. Taking the cap from its box, she stroked it. It felt soft and warm, like a kitten. She rubbed it against the side of her cheek. Her gaze wandered across the room to the window then stretched further again, out to sea. She felt vaguely aware of a strange tingling sensation in her feet. The tingle turned to an itch and suddenly she longed to run ... *must reach it ...*

Sunlight reflected from the surface of the distant water hurting her eyes. She blinked and shook her head. Concentrating now, she folded the cap carefully and placed it inside her coat pocket before heading downstairs. It was early and the house for a pleasant change was quiet. Entering the kitchen, she grabbed a couple of slices of bread from the bread bin and threw them into the toaster. She was just reaching into the fridge for the marmalade when a package to the right caught her eye. A note was attached. It read:

To the earliest bird,
Please take these grenades to Mr Cringle. He's designing
some new launch pins for me. In case you don't know: to
the top paddock, take a right and follow the cliff path
past Ben-Varrey Bay to the first farm. There could be some
pocket money in it!
Mum x

Merryn grabbed the package. The Cringles' farm was on her way. Toast in one hand, grenades in the other, she made her way outside.

Striding across the paddock, she inhaled the morning air. Gusts, fresh from the sea tasted salty on her tongue. The sky was nearly cloudless now. For the first time in a week a smile tugged at the corners of her mouth. She reached the cliff path and skipped. A puffin that hadn't yet departed for warmer shores breezed alongside, its funny-sad harlequin eyes skimming the water for fish. Gulls nesting on the cliff's edge squawked and greeted, their cries carrying across the bay.

Stopping to follow the path of a diving kestrel, her eyes fell to the little patch of shore below: Ben-Varrey Bay, Auntie's favourite swimming spot. Someone was walking from the direction of the water's edge. It was a boy. His hair looked oddly wet, but his clothes and shoes appeared dry. He lifted his head to the sky and shook it. She recognised him. It was Rohan Kelly.

She watched him walk to a clump of rocks by the bay's edge and recover a rucksack. He unzipped it and pushed inside what appeared from a distance to be a grey towel. Not wishing to be seen, she withdrew from the path's edge and continued on her way. As thoughts of school intruded, she pushed them from her mind and concentrated instead on the small flock of sheep grazing on the flat strip of Manx coastline.

A strangled cry from below broke her concentration. Running back to the cliff's edge she looked down. Her hands curled into fists. There were three figures on the beach now. They were locked in some sort of to-ing and fro-ing exercise. The smallest of the three clung to a rucksack. The other two were familiar figures; Huff and Berk.

Clutching Mum's package tightly, she tore down the rocky path to the bay below. By the time she reached the bottom step, Huff had already wrenched the rucksack from Rohan's grasp. Berk had him pinned to the sand and was wrestling with his feet. Sitting on Rohan's chest, he'd managed to remove his shoes and was in the process of pulling off his socks. Rohan struggled, tears of fury streaming down his face. His small frame looked no match for the great lump on top of him.

"Ooohh look, Varney's cryin'," teased Huff. "'E's got no power in the daylight. Let's see what's in the pack. What do yer reckon Berk? Human remains … or more socks?"

Huff ripped open the bag and the grey contents slithered to the ground.

"What the … too gutless to feed off people, eh? Must be suckin' on rats instead. Big rats," he added, poking at what Merryn could now see was a length of fur. Huff picked it up and draped it across his shoulders. It fell into luxurious folds around his body as he pranced about on the sand, baring his teeth and making swooping motions with his arms.

"Verrucas or bat's feet?" shouted Berk in triumph as he ripped a sock from Rohan's foot. Rohan's small fists rained down hard on his back but Berk didn't seem to notice.

"Err, gross!" he cried leaping from Rohan and backing away.

"Freak!" screamed Huff. "Varney's a freak!" Unnerved, he stumbled to the water's edge.

Merryn was close enough to see. *Poor Rohan, no wonder he keeps his socks on!*

"Mutant! Weirdo!" continued Huff, looking shaken.

Then before he could say more, something hit him hard in the centre of the chest. A crimson blotch spread outward. He fell backwards and lay floundering in the freezing water.

Merryn leapt out from her hiding place behind some rocks. "Quick, grab your stuff and follow me," she shouted across to Rohan.

Wading into the sea, Rohan snatched the fur from Huff's shoulders causing him to roll face down into the surf.

"Nice one! This way," urged Merryn.

Grabbing his bag, shoes and socks, Rohan bolted in her direction without looking back.

"Help, I'm dying," coughed Huff, his arms flailing about in the shallow backwash.

"Get up Hafey, yer big wuss," shouted Berk. "It's that O'Reilly scum. It's paint, not blood! Takes a freak to know a freak. Let's get 'em."

"If you can!" hollered Merryn. Tearing up the rocky slope

with Rohan at her heels, she called back to him. "Stay right behind me, close as you can!"

They stumbled onto the coastal path and sprinted away from the bay. The two ran furiously but Merryn sensed the heavy pounding of Huff and Berk drawing ever closer. By the time they'd reached her top paddock, Berk had cut in front and was advancing from the left. He was only a body's length from Rohan's shoulder, when suddenly, Merryn slowed down. Coming to a complete standstill she turned around and watched as the two hurtled towards them. Rohan grabbed her arm and tried to pull her onward.

"No, it's taken care of, really. Just watch … and enjoy."

As Rohan let go, an explosion detonated next to them. Huff and Berk flew backwards and into the air, a deluge of green stuff raining over them. With no time to recover, a second explosion discharged beneath them. It knocked them to the ground covering them in sticky purple paint. Merryn laughed out loud and turned to face Rohan. He looked bewildered and a little frightened.

"My mum, she's a paintball instructor. We're in the minefield. Just stay where you are."

Rohan's jaw dropped. "You're wicked!"

Merryn grinned. "Yeah, I know."

They stood together watching as Huff and Berk, drenched in splatter, triggered explosion after explosion. Finally, humiliated and cowering, the pair reached the edge of the minefield where they had entered, and turned and ran.

Merryn glanced at Rohan's tear-stained face smeared with dirt and flecks of paint and reached into her pocket for a tissue. As the tissue emerged, something fell to the ground — it was the red cap. Rohan took the tissue and began to wipe his face but his eyes never left the cap. Merryn leaned over and scooped it up, folding it back into her pocket.

"Err … it's just a thing … I mean a present … from my late aunt. Not sure what it is."

"I know," said Rohan. "I've seen them before."

"There are others — like this one?"

"Yeah!"

A booming voice cut through their conversation.

"Merryn, is that you? Are you all right? What's going on over there?"

"It's Mum. Gotta go. Can we meet? I need to know more about the cap. I … I think it was important to my aunt."

"Meet me tonight if you can — at the bay. I'll be there at ten-thirty. And Merryn … thanks."

Her cheeks flushed. It had been a while since anyone her own age had thought well of her.

"I hope you don't get into trouble," he added.

"Oh no, Mum hates bullies. I can reset the mines this afternoon."

Waving goodbye and running to her house, she quivered with anticipation. There were more caps out there … just like hers.

Night Swimming

"She raised herself on her beautiful tail
And gave him her soft wet hand:
"I've been long waiting for you, my dear,
Now welcome home from land."
— The Scottish Students' Songbook, 1891

Merryn slipped out of bed and dressed hurriedly in her warmest clothes. She glanced at her bedside clock. It was ten-fifteen. Folding the cap into her pocket, she grabbed a scarf and hat. She nudged open her bedroom door and crept out, tip-toeing along the upstairs landing. Pausing for a moment outside her brothers' shared bedroom, she placed her ear against the closed door and listened. Declan and Dave were still up but sounded pre-occupied — playing a computer game.

Reaching the staircase, she crouched low and peered through the banister. The living room door was open. She heard the thrashing blur of blurple before she saw it. Dad's eyes were closed and he was pounding an air-guitar and singing into a karaoke microphone. The sound was horrible. Merryn cringed. She had perfect pitch and acutely sensitive hearing. In this family it was a curse. Mum was stretched out on the sofa reading a magazine. She didn't seem bothered by the racket.

Treading lightly down the stairs, Merryn slipped out of the back door closing it softly behind. She gazed ahead to the dark horizon thinking about the best way to reach the cliff path. She decided to follow the outer perimeter of both paddocks that ran from the rear of her house, down to the sea. This would mean circumnavigating the minefield, but that shouldn't pose a problem. She'd replanted the mines that afternoon and knew the boundaries well. Still, it was an overcast night with little moonlight to help light the way.

She had her torch but didn't want to risk being seen. Keeping low, she crept along the line of the fence. She skirted around the minefield before stumbling onto the cliff path. Loose stones skipped out from beneath her feet and she took care to stay well back from the cliff's edge. Finally, she made it to the cobbled pathway and used her torch to climb the rest of the way down. She glanced back seeing the lights from her house glowing softly in the distance. Amazingly, she could hear Dad's faint vocals carrying across the paddocks and down to the bay.

"You made it!" Rohan's words came quietly from the dark. She noticed his voice again as she followed the outline of his rucksack to the water's edge. It didn't sound thin like most voices. It was richer, like it had more layers to it.

"Have you got the cap?" he asked.

She glanced in the direction of her coat pocket and gasped. A brilliant ruby glow emanated. She withdrew the cap and held it up. It shimmered and sparkled like a mirror ball, throwing off prisms of red light.

"Wow!" exclaimed Rohan. "I've never seen one this close. Try it on, it wants you to."

Merryn swallowed back the questions that were beginning to line up. She drew the red cap down over her head. The familiar shifting sensation gripped her scalp as the cap glided and shaped to a perfect fit. She gazed across the vast expanse of water and an overwhelming desire to enter it came over her.

"Go on," Rohan urged softly.

"But the cold … my clothes …"

The pull became more powerful. Her feet and legs tingled, then itched and burned. They ached for the cool soothing water. Her protests stopped. She waded into the freezing sea — only it wasn't cold at all. It was … perfect. Questions and impossible thoughts took a back seat as her body and the new sensations took over.

She dived beneath the surface and began a few tentative strokes. In normal circumstances, she was a better than average swimmer. Auntie had coached her from an early age and encouraged her to swim laps across the bay in the summer months. But it had never felt like this. She commanded the water. Spiralling downward and somersaulting, she darted to the right, then the left. Plunging down into the depths, she twisted like a salmon before bursting upward at breakneck speed.

She squealed out loud before gazing across to the shore for Rohan ... only he wasn't there. Suddenly, a dark shape appeared in the water next to her. She felt a stab of fear and slipped quietly below, treading water. She stared at the dark outline. It looked like a seal. Seals swam in these waters occasionally. The silvery shape moved closer before breaking through to the surface. Hesitantly, she followed it upward and as she surfaced, her fear turned to bewilderment. She'd been mistaken. She stared into the face she knew and the impossible thoughts flooded her mind again. *I can swim ... I can see ... I can breathe ... underwater ... So can Rohan.*

Rohan smiled at her shyly. His perfect teeth gleamed in the faint moonlight. He splashed at the surface of the water before somersaulting into the air. The grey fur Merryn had seen earlier in the day was folded over his arm.

She had trouble concentrating. *What's happening?*

"What am I? What are you?" she eventually asked. It sounded feeble but it was all she could manage.

Rohan paused. "I'm not sure. I don't know much myself. What I do know is that your cap and my fur are very magical things."

"Where did your fur come from?"

Suddenly, Rohan looked immensely sad. His dark eyes brimmed over and Merryn knew she'd asked the wrong question.

"We can talk just as well underwater," Rohan blurted. Leaping into the air, he formed a dive before spiralling downward.

She followed the path of froth and bubbles and found to her amazement that she could speak easily under the water. It wasn't at all like the games she played in the local pool with her brothers. They would each hold their breath and take turns at saying the name of a piece of fruit underwater. The others had to guess the type of fruit amongst the deep distorted warbles. Merryn's mouth opened and she projected the right sound, but it was almost as though Rohan could hear her words in his head rather than his ears. She listened to the sound of her own voice, her own breath. It was deeper, richer now, more like Rohan's, like water over rocks, like waves breaking.

"How does the cap work? Where did it come from?" she gushed.

"I'm not sure why your aunt had it, but it's called a *cohuleen druith*." Rohan spoke the unfamiliar words with ease. They sounded natural to him.

"It means enchanted cap, in a very old language. They belong to merrow."

"Merrow! Mermaids! But they're make-believe, fairy tales ..." Merryn paused, reading into Rohan's patient expression. "You mean you've really seen one?"

"Only from a distance mind; they can hide well. The cap works in a similar way to my fur. It must be worn under the water at all times, but merrow can also take human form on land — if they remove their caps."

A great surge of water silenced them. A red-capped, silver-tailed figure appeared suddenly.

"Goggling guppies! What's with the noise? Don't you know about the curfew? These waters are dangerous. Well come on! Follow me."

His voice was so commanding and the message so alarming, they didn't hesitate. A firm hand grasped each of theirs and drew them downward into the murky depths.

"This way, quick, before the green merlitia see us. They're armed, and believe me when I say their trigger fingers are faster than their grey matter!" The merrow tapped the side of his head.

"Excuse me," whispered Rohan, "but what's a merlitia?"

"Merlitia! Oh, they're soldiers … only greener and a lot more stupid. Oops sorry, forgetting myself. Nixter Havmand at your service."

The merrow bowed deeply then smiled, displaying a perfect double row of sharp, white teeth.

He's beautiful! He can't be much older than us.

"Shhh," whispered the merrow as though he could hear her thoughts. "Formalities got to wait. Look — merlitiaman ahead."

Grabbing each of them by the hand again, he pulled them behind a great mound of rock and weed. Then, catching their eyes, he made a swift motion across his mouth that looked as though he were fastening a zip.

Merryn didn't need showing twice. From between the fronds of seaweed, she could just make out a form that, even from a distance, could only be described as pig-ugly. It had a bright green face and body topped with a wild mane of emerald hair. Above a snout of a nose, small eyes were set into a scaly, green face. Inside its mouth were rows of pointy teeth that looked as though they could do with a good brush and floss. Held menacingly under its powerful, flipper-like arm was a three-pronged harpoon.

The green thing looked directly at the pile of rock and weed they were hiding behind. Then, just as Merryn tensed herself ready to bolt, it thrashed its long tail and swam off in the opposite direction.

"Ugly and stupid," murmured Nixter.

"What was it?" whispered Merryn.

"That, I'm awfully sorry to say, was a merrow."

"Do they all look like that?"

"Around here? Yes. Ugly aren't they?"

She nodded her head vigorously. "I always imagined merrow would be beautiful, err, a bit like you in fact." Merryn blushed but Nixter didn't seem to notice.

"Oh, the females are," he replied. "Gorgeous in fact, and can sing like angels. But mermen, ugh!"

"Excuse me," said Rohan again. "I don't mean to be rude, but if that was a merrow then what are you?"

Nixter pulled himself up and puffed out his chest.

"I'm a Scandinavian merrow," he announced proudly. "A superior type altogether. Not that it's appreciated around here." He sniffed loudly. "The females seem to prefer the green variety and the males — humph! Think it amusing to make fun of me. Nerdy Nixter indeed — quite juvenile. Anyway we can't stay here chatting all night. Come on."

They followed him, swimming away from the rocky clump and along the cliff's edge until they reached a small crevice marked by a brass knocker in the shape of a ship's anchor, fixed to one side. Ushered quickly inside, they swam, one by one, through the tight opening to enter a large cavern.

"Welcome to my home," said Nixter.

Merryn let out a small gasp then looked above her head in awe. Clusters of translucent glass fishermen's buoys provided soft lighting. Inside each buoy was a clump of something luminous.

"That's phosphorescent algae," explained Nixter following her gaze. "I cultivate it myself, in my laboratory."

Her eyes made an arc across the room. She swam over to Rohan who was staring at a large, unusual dresser that looked as though it were made entirely from planks and bits of old driftwood.

"I made it … from salvage … off The Titanic," said Nixter proudly.

Suddenly, Merryn looked back across the room and let out a small cry. Nixter was placing a kettle of water on a hob.

"Oh this," he said, pointing to the gas ring. "It's fuelled by natural gas. It burns just as well underwater you know."

"No, begging your pardon," she said, looking down. "It's just … your tail! It's gone!"

Rohan spun around. The two stared at Nixter who stood in the watery kitchen with a pair of legs — real human-like legs encased inside a pair of jeans.

"These?" said Nixter, looking down. "You didn't think I'd have a tail all the time, did you? They're handy for out-seaside, especially if you're in a hurry but a bit unpractical indoors. Always knocking things over and swishing into doorways. Merrow are metamorphic. The red cap allows us to change shape somewhat; but only between human and merrow form.

"Having a red cap means you can have a tail — if you want one," he added. "I can highly recommend them for fast water travel."

"Me? But how?"

"It takes a bit of practice. I'll show you now. Shut your eyes and concentrate on the red cap. You'll need to relax and try to feel it working through your body and down into your legs. Start by taking a deep breath."

Merryn inhaled deeply and allowed her eyelids to drop.

"Good. Now imagine that in place of legs, you have a single flexible limb."

She focused as hard as she could. Slowly, with growing momentum, she felt a strange tingling spill over her head and course down the length of her body. She visualised a tail, strong and powerful. Feeling a curious sensation, she opened her eyes and cried out loud. Her lower body had transformed. Iridescent scales shone in soft shades of lilac, turquoise and green. But in that split second of surprise, her concentration broke and the legs she had always known were instantly back in place. She felt a crippling surge of pain travel down her lower body and grabbed hold of the dresser to steady herself. The pain subsided as quickly as it had come and she let go.

"Err, sorry, forgot to mention that bit," said Nixter. "The transformation is not entirely painless but you'll get used to it with time. It will lessen the more you practice. Well done though and *nice tail!* With a bit more practice you'll have it in no time. The trick is in keeping your concentration in place, but relaxing at the same time."

Nixter turned to Rohan. "As you might already know, for you, transformation is easy. You can take the form of a seal underwater but you're half human and know that state more than any other. You can keep your tail but be human from the waist up by shedding the top half of your fur and securing it around your waist. In order to be fully human you must keep the fur in contact with your body. Place it in a bag or pack and ensure it is attached to your body. You must never release the fur underwater, not even for a minute. If you lose contact with it you will drown."

Rohan gripped the seal skin tightly against his body.

Nixter looked at Merryn again. "The same rule applies to your cap, but even more so." The merrow's eyes locked onto hers. "Your great-aunt, Lorelei Moore, died because of that cap. I'm sure of it. She passed it on to you because she trusted you more than any other. You must guard it with your life."

The Loireag

"Girl of green waters, liquid as lies,
Cool as the calloused snow..."

— Laurie Lee, *Song by the Sea*

"Sorry. Didn't want to shock you but the sooner you know everything the better. You'll have lots of questions but first, let's get comfortable."

Nixter ushered them over to a long wooden table and seated them on what looked to be a couple of old pirates' chests. Their hinged lids were bolted down with metal locks in the shape of skulls and crossbones. They were padded on top and surprisingly soft.

Presently, they were served with mugs of steaming green liquid and a large plate of what looked like pistachio-coloured scones. Merryn screwed her eyes shut then opened them again. Nothing had changed. Here she was in a house under the sea with a merrow and a boy who was half seal — contemplating a midnight snack! The problem was it didn't feel like a weird dream. It felt all too real. She watched as Rohan helped himself to the strange looking food. *He's used to this.*

"Excuse me," said Rohan, "but how do you stop the food from going soggy and the tea from running away?"

"A great invention called Antisag," replied Nixter. "It works on the ingredients at a cellular level by proofing the cell walls and making them impervious to water. Its second function is to bind the cells strongly together so that the seawater doesn't separate the food or liquid particles and wash them away. Before Antisag, eating was so boring — lots of sitting about chewing on kelp. It's revolutionised merrow cuisine.

"It was actually a great-uncle of mine who invented it. I don't want to sound conceited, but we Scandinavian merrow pride ourselves on being well schooled. What we lack in green brawn, we make up for with intellect. I hold degrees in both Marine Medicine and Forensic Science."

"Medicine and science … but you can't be much older than us!" exclaimed Rohan.

"One hundred and twenty-four is plenty old enough to pack in a bit of study!" announced Nixter. "Of course it helps being smart. Don't look too surprised. Merrow live for ages. Eight hundred years isn't uncommon." Nixter scratched his head. "In human terms, I guess that makes me about fourteen."

Suddenly, Merryn gasped out loud. "We haven't introduced ourselves! I'm Merryn O'Reilly and this is Rohan Kelly." She braced herself. "What happened to Auntie?"

Nixter's flawless face softened. He placed his mug down on the table.

"Anatomically speaking, Lorelei died of a heart attack. I examined her immediately after her death — before your examiners reached her. There was no sign of any damage to her body nor that there had been a struggle."

Merryn interrupted again. "Auntie swam every day. She was fit and strong. She could beat both my brothers at arm wrestling and out-swim them any day of the week."

"I agree," said Nixter staring down at the table. "I hate to be the one to tell you, you obviously cared for her very much. But, I don't believe your aunt died an entirely natural death. I could tell from her … expression." He looked up again and leaned forward gripping the table. "Something frightened her. Something frightened her so badly her heart stopped beating."

Merryn listened to the water swirling around the cavern. She felt her own heart pound.

"We in the underwater world were shocked. She was a frequent visitor here. Her death was a major part of the reason to bring about a curfew. She spoke with our community just over a week ago. She wanted to pass on the *cohuleen druith* to a younger guardian, her grand-niece. This request was met with approval … and much sadness. Unfortunately, although your aunt possessed the cap, she was mortal and growing older much more quickly than we merrow. She felt she could no longer confidently care for it."

"You hinted that Aunt Lorelei's death was only part of the reason for the curfew," said Merryn. "What was the other?"

"A horrible crime," said Nixter, shuddering. "Fortunately though, one that didn't succeed. A couple of days before Lorelei's death, someone tried to break into Merling House — our baby hospital — and steal the red cap from a baby. This is the most heinous of crimes. To steal the cap from a baby merrow means to end its life. To kill an adult is wicked enough, but to kill a baby for personal gain …"

Nixter's golden skin paled and his slender hands trembled.

"Who would do that?" cried Merryn.

For a moment Nixter was silent. His head turned slowly and he gazed upwards to a small plaque above the opening to his home. Merryn followed the line of his eyes, surprised she hadn't noticed the sign before. Curiosity growing, she read the following:

UNDERWATER DETECTIVE AGENCY
Proprietor: Nixter Havmand, BMedSci, DFM, DPath

"I don't know," said Nixter. His hands gripped even harder around the edges of the table. "But I'm just the merrow to find out." He paused for a moment before suddenly, his eyes popped open wide.

"Hey, I don't suppose you'd like to help, would you? Three heads are much better than one, even one as brilliant as mine."

"I'm already there!" cried Merryn instantly. The strange dream-like night suddenly felt incredibly normal. To pull herself back into Auntie's world again, to help her in any way she could was something she'd never need to think about. "Yes please!"

"Count me in," added Rohan quickly.

"Excellent!" exclaimed Nixter, clapping his hands together. "When can we start?"

Silence filled the water. Finally it was Rohan who broke it.

"Err, we've been down here for a while now and our parents don't know we're gone. We should head back, for now at least."

"We could come again, this weekend," said Merryn. Rohan nodded vigorously.

Nixter stood up. "Sounds like a plan. I've talked enough for one night. I'll lead you back to the bay now. Remember the curfew is still in place. You must stay close by me. It's been great meeting you both."

Against her will, Merryn dragged herself up. Her throat suddenly felt sore and tight — choking on questions. She helped Nixter and Rohan clear away the tea dishes. *If this place was real, what else was real?*

"Do faeries really exist?" she blurted out.

Nixter turned around. He paused, seeming surprised by the question.

"Like me you mean?" he said eventually.

"I guess," said Merryn. The confusion and strangeness of the night overwhelmed her again. She sank down onto a chest.

"Infinite varieties exist," said Nixter gently. "Some, like myself, dwell in water. Some dwell on land, some in air and some rare creatures can come to life in fire. I guess it would be easier for you to think of them as elements of nature. They are the wind in your hair — the sand between your toes — the snowflakes on your eyelashes — the fire in your hearth. Most faeries exist in other realms. Humans can't always see them and, as time passes, this is becoming more so. Our presence was once an important part of yours — beings of light and spirit, and water and earth, reminded humans that their bond with nature was a vital one.

"I don't mean to come over all preachy but, sadly, modern humans seen to have forgotten this. The link between your world and ours is slipping away. Only a hundred years ago it was still common, especially in this part of the world, for humans to commune with faeries. Rituals of respect, such as leaving a small token of appreciation for them on the hearth before bed, or not chopping down a tree that was known to be sacred to them, were commonplace. Some special individuals, who feel a deep connection with nature and can open their hearts to its magic, will always find us, but these rare souls are now few and far between."

Nixter rested his hand lightly on Merryn's shoulder. "Enough for tonight. You should return home now and rest. You've had much to absorb."

Merryn nodded and stood up slowly. Suddenly, Nixter had a tail again. He swam to his front door and peered out. "The way's clear. Let's go now."

Merryn and Rohan swam to his side and followed him cautiously out of the cave. They'd barely swum two hundred yards when they stopped abruptly. Between themselves and the main body of water that led to Ben-Varrey Bay, were two soldiers. Nixter quickly ushered them back to the rock crevice that led to his house and spoke quietly.

"Those big green fellows don't look as though they'll be going anywhere in a hurry. The problem with swimming around them is that it could take some time and we're bound to run into more merlitia along the way. Once we leave the safety of the cliff, we'll be exposed and there are few places to hide. There's an alternative route but it could be dangerous. Behind my house is a passageway that channels through rock and exits at a blowhole."

"I know the blowhole," said Merryn. "It borders our property. I don't think we could climb it. It sprays out big jets of water most of the time."

"If we get the timing right it might be possible," said Nixter. "It's currently low tide. The blowhole is only a few feet deep and the sides are craggy and ridged — ideal for getting a good foothold. If we hurry, the water level will be below the start of the hole. It should be possible to climb up."

"What are we waiting for?" exclaimed Rohan.

"Let's do it," agreed Merryn. The thought of dodging more merlitia was not attractive.

"Wait!" said Nixter. "It's not the blowhole I'm worried about; it's the tunnel. I haven't been inside it for years. I don't know whether it's safe."

Merryn detected a note of fear in Nixter's voice. "What's bothering you?" she asked.

"Well, it might be my imagination, but recently I've heard an unusual noise … coming from the tunnel. It burrows behind my house and passes close to the living room wall."

"What sort of noise?" asked Rohan.

"A strange sound, a bit like wailing, only higher pitched. Most of the time I think I must be imagining it. The sea can make odd noises. I used to think it might be air and water rushing through the passageway, drawn along by currents. But the sound never seems to correspond with the tides, as it should."

Merryn looked up suddenly and tensed herself. She tapped Nixter on the shoulder, compelling him to look around. Two harpoons were pointing in their direction.

"Quickly!" exclaimed Nixter. "Follow me!"

He led them downward, directly below his house. Hidden beneath a rocky ledge was a large metal grill. It was ornate and fanned out in the shape of a scallop. Nixter reached deep inside his pocket and drew out a big brass key. Inserting this into a great, rusty lock, he turned it as hard and as fast as he could. The lock didn't budge.

Merryn looked up to see the two merlitiamen taking aim.

"Hurry!" she urged.

Nixter twisted the key hard in the opposite direction and, to Merryn's enormous relief, she heard the sound of hinges creaking and groaning. Nixter pushed them through the opening and swiftly locked the gate behind. A loud 'thwack' followed by the echo of metal rebounding, sounded behind them as the first harpoon struck the gate. A second sailed through a gap in the bars. It impacted with the rocky surface at the side of the tunnel's entrance. They swam into a narrow opening and were guided sharply upward and to the right.

"Phew, that was close," said Nixter. "I doubt they'll follow us. This tunnel is part of my property and we're no longer trespassing in public waters. We have to hurry, though. The tide is turning faster than I'd anticipated. We need to reach the blowhole as soon as possible."

"It's awfully dark," whispered Merryn.

"Yes, and in my haste, I haven't brought a light source. We'll have to feel our way along the sides of the tunnel. It's important we stay together. I'll take the lead. Rohan, stay behind me with Merryn at the rear. If you sense you've drifted, call out and we'll regroup."

Gingerly, Merryn inched forward, her hands trailing across the slimy passage walls. Nixter's voice echoed from ahead.

"We must hurry. I can feel the water quickening. It's vital we reach the blowhole before it begins to surge."

Suddenly, from the depths of the tunnel ahead, came an eerie noise. It sounded like the cry of a baby but deeper, less natural somehow. Merryn groped ahead of her and clutched at Rohan's rucksack. She hoped he couldn't feel her hands shaking. The strange sound petered out. Just the swirling and lapping of water could be heard now. She was beginning to feel a bit weak. Still clutching Rohan's pack, she allowed it to haul her along. They continued on like this for a few yards when the sound began again, only this time its quality changed. The pitch rose sharply and escalated, peaking in a high, blood-curdling screech.

"W ... what was that?" Merryn stammered.

"I ... I don't know but it doesn't sound much like air or sea," gulped Nixter. "But turning back now could be more dangerous than taking our chances with what lies ahead. The merlitia will not leave the tunnel entrance until the curfew ends; this much I know. We could retreat and wait by the gate until their shift ends at dawn, but you'll not reach your homes before daybreak."

"My parents would kill me," said Merryn.

"Dad's an early riser, he checks on me first thing," added Rohan. "Dad worries ... a lot. If he finds me gone ..."

"Then we'll take our chances with what lies ahead. Be brave. Keep close to me and do exactly as I say. If I tell you to swim ahead, you must find the blowhole yourselves and exit as quickly as you can. The noise has stopped for now; let's press on."

Feeling for the side of the tunnel Merryn pushed herself forward. The water current had strengthened somewhat in the right direction helping to speed them along. Suddenly, without warning, Nixter stopped moving. Like a line of carts hitting a wall, Rohan bumped into him, then Merryn into Rohan.

"What is it?" cried Rohan.

"It's the tunnel wall, there's a big hole here!" exclaimed Nixter. "I don't remember there being a gap in the wall at any point. This space seems to be another opening altogether. I've no recollection of any other passageways down here, but it's been many years since I last visited. Let's hold hands and form a line. We'll veer to the right and see if our passageway continues."

After some bumping and groping they finally located the blowhole. The current was strong now and Merryn could feel the water thrusting in explosive gusts. All of a sudden, she shrieked out loud. Something had caught hold of her long hair and was coiling it sharply around like a line of rope. Immobilised, her fear escalated as a nasty hissing sounded in her ear.

"Ye'll not be getting by without a wee *toon*."

The hideous screech that followed was deafening. Writhing in pain, Merryn tried to pull free, but the lock on her head was too powerful. Then she remembered something — inside her left pocket was the torch. One hand gripped Rohan's rucksack but the other was free. She groped about and managed to locate it. She thrust it forward in Rohan's direction.

"A torch ... I've got one ... its waterproof ... here ... take it!"

Her grip on the rucksack broke. Moments later the torch left her grasp and the watery passage lit up.

The first thing Merryn noticed was Rohan biting his cheek, as if to stop himself from screaming. She managed to twist her head slightly to one side then wished she hadn't. Alongside her, hair coiled tightly in its claw-like hand, stood a creature, vaguely human and so horrible, she thought she'd entered a nightmare. The thing was tall, thin and stooped. Bluish-hued skin sagged from its face and body in long folds. But it was the eyes that frightened her the most. She'd gazed into them for a moment. They had no irises and no whites — just black holes. They couldn't be read. She looked urgently to Nixter and dared to speak.

"Wh … what is it?"

"A loireag."

Nixter pronounced the word lorryack. He continued to speak as though it wasn't there, probably in an effort to keep her calm.

"They're a malignant water spirit. Usually, they keep to themselves, but something has upset this one badly, and for quite some time judging from the wails I've been hearing. They can be extremely nasty if rubbed up the wrong way."

"What would upset them?" stammered Rohan.

"In the faerie world, they preside over two things: sewing and singing. If someone does not give proper care and attention to the making, washing and care of garments or, worse still, sings in a harsh or tuneless voice, they will become riled."

Merryn knew at once what had upset the loireag.

"Dad," she whispered.

The loireag let loose a blood curdling screech. Merryn's body jolted as more hissing followed.

"Her kin makes the terrible racket!"

Merryn winced as the loireag's teeth grazed the tender skin of her throat.

"Quickly," cried Rohan. "What can we do?"

"Only beautiful music will soothe her now, and I have none to offer," said Nixter helplessly.

Merryn watched as Nixter and Rohan swam bravely forward. Then she opened her mouth stopping them in mid-stroke. A sound — her perfectly pitched gorgeous sound, built slowly, then soared. She opened her mouth wider allowing notes of utter perfection to pour out until a melody formed. The loireag closed her eyes. Slowly, her body relaxed and Merryn's hair uncoiled, slipping from the claws.

"Coming from the lips of a human," whispered Nixter. "Who would have thought?"

Inching forward, Merryn continued to sing. She gestured for the others to follow. With the strong current and the torch lighting their way, they made quick progress. Merryn's song was coming to a close. She glanced back in the faint light to see the loireag relaxed and motionless just as they reached the rocky base of a great hole.

Nixter spoke quickly as they bobbed up and down in the powerful current. "The water is coursing strongly. You can't climb up. Keep your cap and fur in place. You must wait for a strong surge and ride it upwards. Stay together. The opening narrows at the top and you may be in for a bumpy ride. Good luck. I won't come with you — I'll wait with the loireag. She's soothed. If she stirs, I'll show her my attire. I never neglect my washing!" He pulled himself up proudly.

"You must go. It was wonderful meeting you both. Come again, as soon as you can. I need to show you Marrey Turris."

"What's Marrey Turris?" asked Merryn.

"Who's Marrey Turris?" said Rohan at exactly the same time.

"It's the capital of my world, a sub-aqueous palace and grounds —though we call it Turrey most of the time."

Nixter swished his long tail and was gone.

Merryn waited with Rohan at the base of the blowhole. As the swell increased, they locked hands and caught a tremendous surge, surfing it upward. They scraped and bumped a little towards the top but it was easier than expected. With Rohan at her side, she hauled herself over the edge.

Cap and fur safely tucked away, they walked without speaking until they reached the outer edge of the paddock that led to Merryn's house. She stopped and looked at Rohan, struggling to find words to express what they had just shared.

"Try not to think about it too much," he said. His soft rich voice was soothing. "That works for me. Some things just are."

Merryn felt lighter. *Why struggle?* She found her voice. "Exciting night, wasn't it?"

"Too right, specially the last bit. Exciting and scary! Thanks for saving our skins. Your voice is awesome."

Merryn blushed. "I was pretty scared too."

"See you at school on Monday then?"

"Can't wait!"

She grinned and waved, watching Rohan until he was out of sight. Walking back to her house she reflected on her incredible day. She'd managed to outsmart two bullies, solve the mystery of the cap, discover an underwater world, overcome a nasty water sprite and make a friend. No, two friends. Nixter had invited them back. *Don't struggle, some things just are …*

She reached the back door. Pulling it slowly and quietly ajar, she revealed, not the passageway leading to the staircase, but a stony-faced Mum and Dad.

Ben-Varrey Boulevard of Beauty

Turrey

"Up from Aegean caverns, pool by pool
Of blue salt sea, where feet most beautiful
Of Nereid maidens weave beneath the foam
Their long sea-dances …"

— Euripides, *The Trojan Woman*

What if they ground me … worse … confiscate the cap? The thought was unbearable. Her voice had managed to get her out of trouble once that night; she must try again. She glanced bravely upwards until her eyes connected with Mum's. Taking in the deeply furrowed brow and tight, thin line of a mouth, she quickly looked down again. Suddenly a loireag didn't seem quite so scary.

"You're in deep trouble young lady. Your father and I have been worried sick! We were on the verge of calling PC Quirk. Where have you been? Don't leave anything out and make sure it's the truth we're hearing … the whole truth … or so help me …"

"That'll do Shaz, give the kid a chance!" said Dad. "Now, what's yer story miss? Splitting the house … an ungodly hour of the night … no note … no message … no nothing. For all we knew yer could have bin lying in a ditch frozen to death, kidnapped, or worse. Well, come on … spill the juice! Haven't got all night!"

Merryn's thoughts raced. The truth would not be helpful. Mum and Dad wouldn't be calling Quirk, they'd be calling Dr Fayle.

"Err … sorry … really. It's just … um … I … think I must have been sleep walking. All I know is that I woke up outside. How I got there …"

Merryn shrugged her shoulders then lowered her head ashamed of the lie. She might have been the silver-tongued star of the evening but she wasn't perfect.

She glanced up. Dad's face had softened somewhat but Mum looked at her suspiciously.

"Yeah, sleep walking with your clothes on … and a torch. To bed now, and don't let's find you out of it again."

Merryn couldn't believe she'd got off so lightly. She would have to be much more careful in planning future excursions.

She hurried into her dark bedroom and pulling her clothes off, she found her pyjamas and tugged them on. She placed the torch on her bedside dresser and located her favourite book, the one Auntie had given her. Jumping into bed, she grabbed the torch and burrowed deep beneath the covers. She opened the book and shone the light onto the index page. Thumbing to a chapter titled *Myths and Legends,* she quickly scanned a couple of pages until she found the passage she was looking for. She read the following:

"The Selkie or Roane is a type of faerie seal peculiar to the great grey and crested seal families. They are metamorphic creatures and possess great magic. By removing their outer skin, they can transform into humans on land and live a normal human life if desired. However, the Selkie will always have a powerful draw to the sea, and the union of a human and a Selkie will usually end in the Selkie returning to the sea, even if this means leaving loved ones. The children of such a marriage will frequently have webbed hands or feet."

It was Friday lunchtime, and Merryn sat in a far corner of the canteen opposite Rohan.

"Did you see Huff and Berk today?" she whispered.

"Yeah, they didn't look at me once," replied Rohan. "What do you think they're up to?

"Who cares? We've got much better things to think about. What are you doing tomorrow morning? Shall we meet at the bay, about ten o'clock? We'll do a day swim if that's okay. If Mum and Dad catch me sleep walking again, I'm doomed."

Saturday morning arrived and Merryn gulped down her breakfast.

"Mum, can I have the morning off munitions duty?"

"Mmmm, I'll have to negotiate a pocket money drop. What pressing engagements do you have?"

"I've got a new friend."

Mum's face lit up. "Why didn't you say so? Girl or boy?"

"Err, boy. Thanks Mum, gotta go. Be back after lunch." Merryn grabbed a piece of toast and bolted for the back door.

"Ooh Merryn, what's his name …?"

She closed the door quickly behind her. The cold wind nipped at her cheeks as she tore down the length of the paddocks. Slowing to a trot, she made her way along the cliff path. Rohan was heading towards her in the opposite direction. She waited for them to meet up. Together, they followed the rocky steps down to the bay, taking care they were not followed.

"Do you live near here?" Merryn asked.

"Dad and I live in the old farm house, just over there." Rohan stopped to point. "It's on the Cringle's property. Dad works for Mr Cringle." Rohan secured his rucksack and strode out into the freezing water.

Merryn's face lit up. "Get out! We're practically neighbours." She jumped up and down excitedly, pulling her cap on. Casting a last backward glance at the beach, she eagerly entered the sea.

The water felt every bit as delicious as last time. She spiralled downward, noting, just as on land, how different things looked in the daylight. The weak late-November sun penetrated the depths, casting an enchanting pale-green light all around. Merryn shut her eyes and rubbed them for a moment before opening up again. Seeing underwater with a red cap on was like looking through a kaleidoscope full of diamonds. Every surface sparkled and glistened, reflecting prisms of rainbow-coloured light. Colours seemed brighter — more alive and intense. She easily recognised familiar landmarks from the previous weekend: the clump of emerald seaweed, the silvery rock they had hidden behind and the brass anchor glittering at the side of the crevice leading to Nixter's house.

Following behind Rohan, she watched as he struck the knocker twice. A shout of "enter" was quickly returned and they swam inside. Nixter was clearly expecting them. The table was laid for three and the kettle was boiling away on the hob. She glanced around the beautiful cavern taking in the well-ordered neatness.

"Come in." Nixter turned from his position in the kitchen and smiled at them. Merryn's throat suddenly tightened. Nixter was the most extraordinary and beautiful thing she had ever seen. He was how she imagined an angel might look. He had luminous golden skin like the sun and the most incredible eyes. They were like cats' eyes — shiny and curious but much warmer. They were the exact colour of a picture she had once seen of the Caribbean Sea — a startling shade of turquoise.

"Glad you made it home safely last week," Nixter said. "Come and sit down." He fussed away and soon they were seated around the table with a delicious assortment spread out in front of them. Rohan didn't hesitate. He piled his plate high with miniature blue 'sausages' (an old recipe of Nixter's mother), and used some of the freshly baked scone-like things Merryn had seen the previous week, to make hot dogs. Gingerly, Merryn took one of each and assembled them in the same way as Rohan before taking a cautious bite. Pausing only for a second, she crammed the whole thing into her mouth at once. It tasted unbelievable! Delicious! The flavours were sort of what she'd expect from similar looking human food only louder and stronger and they lingered in her mouth long after the food had been chewed and swallowed. Nixter was an amazing cook.

As she grabbed more food, Nixter began to discuss the events of the previous weekend. First, he told them what had happened in the tunnel after they parted ways.

"I had to wait a few hours for the curfew to end. As I suspected, merlitia guarded at the tunnel entrance until dawn. The loireag was no trouble. She stirred once or twice but the sight of my freshly pressed clothes relaxed her. I wanted to explore that second passageway but didn't think it would be a good idea alone and unarmed. I examined the surface stone at the entrance — it seems newly hewn. Strange stuff, but the presence of a loireag is equally odd. They prefer fresh-water as a rule, and don't hang around places where music ... err ... of low quality is a common occurrence. My apologies ..."

"No offence taken." Merryn laughed. "He's pretty awful, isn't he?"

"I've had occasion to muffle my ears if I'm up that way. But back to the loireag … The fact she hasn't moved is disturbing. It's as though she's guarding that passage. Although now I'm saying it, it seems ridiculous. Loireags can't be commanded."

They were silent for a few moments then Nixter praised Merryn on her singing ability.

"You definitely saved us. They're nasty creatures, loireags. Your voice could put some of our finest merrow to shame!"

"Yeah, I surprised myself. My voice is okay, for a person that is, but it's never sounded like that. I think the cap somehow gave me extra ability."

Nixter nodded vigorously before announcing his plans for the day.

"Let's go to Turrey. It's worth seeing for the palace alone but, there's also someone I'd like you to meet. And before I forget …" Nixter walked to a nearby table and picked up a folded length of yellow stuff. "This is the *Turrey Tribune*. I've advertised!" He opened the strange looking *paper* to a section towards the back and handed it to them. It felt stiff and coarse, like dry seaweed and was covered in dark-green writing. Merryn and Rohan held it between them and read the following:

UNDERWATER DETECTIVE AGENCY
Proprietor: Nixter Havmand, BMedSci, DFM, DPath
Assistants: Merryn O'Reilly and Rohan Kelly
The Cliffside, Ben-Varrey Bay

Any mystery fathoms deep,
Don't wring your hands, or fret or weep,
Just let us know, we're here to help,
We know our seaweed from our kelp.
We see clues too small for most,
In all our waters, coast to coast.
With lamprey eyes and dog fish nose,
We'll rid you of your mystery woes.

Giving them just enough time to read, Nixter began to explain. "I don't expect we'll be inundated at first, just the odd case here and there until word gets around. But, what better way to find out if anything out of the ordinary is going on around here, than inviting information." He looked directly at the top of Merryn's head. "As I said before, I believe your aunt's death had something to do with her cap. Her decision to pass the cap on was sudden and unexpected. Lorelei was no frail old lady! I think she felt deeply threatened. The same week someone tried to steal a cap from a baby ... unheard of in our world ... unthinkable. Are the two incidents related? I think they are.

"Let's begin in Turrey. Our first task is to find out how your aunt came to have a red cap."

The three tidied up and prepared for the journey. Curiously, Nixter pulled from a shelf in his kitchen, what looked like a large cake tin. He placed it in a bag which he slung over his shoulder.

Merryn showed off the result of a week's worth of practice;

a beautiful tail and one she could summon at will. Then she watched as Rohan withdrew the fur from the rucksack he wore on his back and pulled it up, securing it at the waist. The transformation from boy to part selkie was graceful. She tingled all over. *What an amazing world I've entered.*

Together, the three set off. Nixter led them out to deeper sea before taking a downward turn. Eventually, they reached a large body of dark water surrounded by a deep shelf of rock and coral.

"This is the Black Hole. Turrey lies at its base. Most of the merrow community lives in or around Turrey. I like to reside further out. Scandinavian merrow prefer the coastline. We like cliffs and rocky outcrops, they somehow seem cosier."

Merryn swam closer to the rim and peered down. Way below them something large glimmered. She followed Nixter and Rohan downwards, all the time coming closer to a vast semi-translucent mass. Eventually, they reached what appeared to be the peaked tip of a turret. From what she could see, it was one of four. Its rounded column was constructed of clear aqua glass, and from the distance, it looked like a massive ice sculpture.

The turrets were incredibly tall and they swam a long way before reaching the crenellated walls of Turrey Palace. Once there, they followed the glass surface around until they reached a set of massive wrought-silver gates. Two fierce-looking soldiers of the green variety guarded the entrance. On seeing Nixter they nodded and promptly opened up.

As the gates clanked shut behind them, the three swam

into an ornate courtyard. Its vast floor was paved in a mosaic made of lustrous pearl shell in shades of blue, lilac, pink and green. Mesmerised, it was a while before Merryn could lift her eyes from the mosaic and look around. The first thing she noticed was that each of the towers was completely different.

Nixter seemed to read her mind.

"The south-east turret is the present ruler, Lir's, private quarters. The south-west turret houses our educational institutions and includes a very fine library. The back two towers are more interesting. The one on the right is dedicated to the female of our species and the one on the left to the male. Call the arrangement old-fashioned, but this is how it has always been."

This seemed to explain the differences in appearance and atmosphere between them. Swimming to the back left tower, Merryn stood at the base of a central spiral staircase and peered up. Her breath caught as she spied immense glass-walled arcades glinting in soft shades of aqua and turquoise. Exquisite-looking creatures glided along, chattering and singing.

"Would you like to go up?" inquired Nixter.

"Can we all enter?"

"Why yes. No one's ever excluded from a tower; it's just that mermen are not remotely interested in female pursuits and vice versa. Come on." They traversed the main staircase and entered into a nearby arcade. Its entrance was framed with a finely wrought, metal arch, which read in silver letters,

Ben-Varrey Boulevard of Beauty. Electric-blue fish darted in and out of the metal work.

"Look, it's named after our little bay!" exclaimed Merryn.

"Ben-Varrey once meant merrow in these parts," explained Nixter. Swimming along for a few metres, they came to a doorway. Merryn paused to read a sign out the front. It said *Cohuleen Couture*. She swam to a nearby window and peered inside. Every surface of the spacious interior was decorated with a vast number of incredibly colourful pieces of jewellery; everything from exotic-looking fish set with colourful gems to enamelled ladybirds.

"The decorations are used by female merrow — to personalise their red caps," explained Nixter. "Most merrow select and use the same motif for life. The symbol becomes an insignia of sorts, something that identifies them. Choosing the right motif is a serious business."

Suddenly, the patron of *Cohuleen Coture* darted out of the shop. She studied Merryn closely before introducing herself. She had flaming red hair and almond-shaped green eyes. A large jewelled spider was attached to the side of her cap.

"I'm Madame Angelaqua. This is my house." The green eyes narrowed. "You have an unadorned cap. It is rare. The cap looks second-hand."

Madame Angelaqua looked as though she had just sniffed something most unpleasant.

"Come inside."

It was a command rather than a request and Merryn followed her at once. She hovered near the entrance and watched as Madame's eyes scanned the walls looking back to her occasionally.

"Forgive my being personal. It's a necessary part of the job. Now, you look harmless enough but gutsy I think." Madame frowned, obviously finding this trait most uncomely. She leaned forward continuing her scrutiny.

"The cap has seen more than one lifetime; very uncommon. Still, it is a desirable cap, desired greatly I think. Green will remind you of this. I have just the thing."

She swam to the rear wall and unclipped a small brooch in the shape of a shamrock. It was cast from green metal and set with brilliantly cut emerald gems. It gleamed and sparkled as water rippled across its surface. Merryn thought it most beautiful.

Madame leaned over and pinned it to the side of her cap.

"Perfect," she purred. "Shamrock is of the earth. It's hardy and flourishes in most parts. It's also considered lucky. You have these qualities I feel, but one can never have too much."

She turned to Nixter. "That will be a jar of your best elixir Dr Havmand. You may deliver it anytime."

Nixter smiled at Madame and nodded.

"You may go now," she said dismissing them. She was already looking out for her next customer.

They floated back down, Nixter urging them towards the right tower. Along the way Merryn stopped briefly to peer inside the window of an establishment called *Spa Tropicana*. She saw waterfalls, lush green foliage and a small artificial beach complete with palm trees. Merrow basked on rocks carefully arranged to show off their long lustrous tails. A large sign advertised treatments such as scale polishing and seaweed wraps. The spa looked very inviting and she longed to enter.

Nixter pulled at her arm, breaking the trance and eventually they drifted back down the stairs arriving at the north-east edge of the palace.

Stark and unadorned, it contrasted greatly with the previous tower block. Merryn looked around and quickly concluded that sport seemed to be the favoured past-time of mermen. A large poster on the wall advertised a forthcoming match of a pursuit called Trimetta. From the picture of a group of burly merrow tackling a ball with tridents, it looked like a highly dangerous version of water polo.

Making their way back to the central courtyard, they were suddenly accosted. A uniformed merman balanced a silver tray, upon which perched a formal-looking white card. He was flanked on either side by two young females, incredibly even lovelier than those they had already seen. Merryn noticed that they both wore the same tiny enamelled bluebird motif on the sides of their caps.

"Those are sirens," whispered Nixter. "Sirens are singled out by their exceptional voices. I think we're about to receive the invitation we require."

The merman picked up the card and held it aloft. The sirens opened their mouths and an exquisite sound pitched forth. In perfect harmony, they sang:

Dr Havmand and his friends,
Are most welcome to my dens.
Lir's heart would soar with great delight,
If you should loom before my sight.
For tea and treats most divine,
A sip of water, a glass of wine.
So come, please come, no excuses make,
And Nixter, I hope you've brought some cake!

Nixter laughed out loud at this last line and patted his bag.

"I certainly have! Come my friends, we're about to meet the King of Marrey Turris!"

The sirens wove an arm around Merryn and Rohan and led them across the courtyard and into the palace headquarters. Inside, a silver spiral staircase rose upwards through the centre of the tower until it disappeared out of sight. The uniformed merrow explained that Lir's private rooms, where he received guests, were situated at the very top of the tower and that it would be best to take the lift. They entered a silver cage at the outer glass edge of the tower.

As the lift rose upward, they had a clear view of the vast sea around them. All manner of wondrous sea creatures drifted and darted about. One species of fish in particular, seemed most prolific. Nixter, a slight frown on his face, caught the eye of the uniformed merrow.

"Cod," they announced in unison.

"Most unusual," said the merrow.

"Precisely," answered Nixter. 'We are a little far south to

attract cod in these waters. They must be holding a gathering of sorts."

Rohan suddenly changed the subject and the cod were forgotten.

"What's Lir like?" he asked.

Nixter laughed out loud. "Wait and see. I will tell you that he has reigned in Turrey for over eight hundred years."

Finally, the lift stopped and they stepped out into a large circular room at the top of the turret. Merryn followed behind Nixter and Rohan to the room's centre, approaching what appeared from a distance to be an enormous circular mirror. On closer inspection they saw that it was actually a pond. Strangely, within the body of water that surrounded them, lay a pool of darker water, the colour of ink. It was contained within a vast onyx dish.

As she gazed into it, tiny starbursts of light ignited from the base of the pond to form a perfect map of some constellations of the northern hemisphere.

"Look, there's Pegasus!" exclaimed Rohan.

A quiet voice spoke from behind. "Impressive, isn't it? I'll show you how it works."

Before they could turn around, a spotlight shone down from above, iluminating the pool of midnight blue. The map of stars disappeared and in its place were literally thousands of the most incredibly small and ferocious-looking fish. They were unnervingly ugly with sharp fang-like teeth set into dog-jawed mouths. Antennae grew out of the tops of their heads and curved over with what appeared to be tiny light bulbs at the end of each tip. The fish were momentarily stunned and blinked in the glare of the light.

"Sorry, guys," said the voice to the fish. The spotlight snapped off and the pool was dark again.

The guests turned around to face a young boy of about their own age. He had short dark hair, a smattering of freckles across his nose and eyes the same inky colour as the pool. The dark eyes were hard to read but twinkled with kindness and warmth.

"They are deep sea anglers, also known as black devil fish," the boy explained. "Their dorsal spines are tipped with light-producing organs called photophores. They are able to produce chemicals that create artificial light through a process known as bioluminescence. Each of these fish represents a star or group of stars from the Northern hemisphere's night sky. They have been trained to map the progress of their particular star or star cluster, throughout the year, and move accordingly. The study of the movement of stars is an old method of divination and one we merrow find to be surprisingly accurate. My little friends here can also show you the southern hemisphere. He snapped his fingers in the air twice and the dark pool became a mass of movement. Tiny lights darted here and there, then suddenly became still.

"There's the Southern Cross," cried Merryn. She turned to face the boy. "Is Lir your grandfather?"

Quickly, she realised her mistake. The boy in front of her had spoken intelligently, like an adult. He had an air of authority about him and an openness that promised honesty.

These were the traits of a leader. The boy before her was Lir, ruler of Turrey. She apologised quickly for her error and the boy laughed.

"You were expecting a salty old seadog, weren't you? Come on!"

Merryn and Rohan joined his laughter.

"I fool almost everyone the first time. It often comes in handy when meeting dignitaries from the international sea community. I'm frequently underestimated — but only once. It's true, I do look much younger than merrow of my age and they have long lives. But gods once ruled these oceans and it is from them I am descended. However, I'm also part merrow. I will age eventually, but a great deal more slowly than most.

"Now, to more important matters. Nixter, have you brought any cake?"

Suddenly he was a child again and Merryn realised that she liked this mer-king/boy immensely. She sensed the same feeling in Rohan's broad smile.

"Nixter is the most marvellous cook. I don't get to sample his work nearly enough. He thinks I'll become distracted from my duties, and he's probably right." Lir sighed. "Most of my work is deadly serious. I'd love to play a little more, but duty is duty. A lot of people rely on me and I don't like to let them down. All the same …" He looked at them enviously, but only for a moment.

"You must be Lorelei's grand-niece, I recognise the cap. And your friend, you have the look of Nuala."

Rohan nodded. "I'm Rohan Kelly."

Lir took Rohan's hand and squeezed it.

"Please, come and be seated."

Lir led them to a low table surrounded by cushions in the shape of starfish. As Merryn seated herself, two doors opened. In swam a couple of merrow carrying trays. They placed a large glass of pale-green liquid in front of each guest and retreated. Bubbles rose from the tops of the glasses and suddenly the water smelt intoxicating.

"We call it anemone ale," explained Lir. "It's made from anemone juice and sea grapes. Try it, please."

Merryn took a tentative sip then had to hold herself back from downing the lot in one mouthful. At the same time Nixter opened his bag and pulled out the tin from his kitchen. He took off the lid to reveal an exquisite-looking cake. It was covered in mint-green icing and decorated with icing starfish in a darker shade of green. Lir's face lit up and Merryn's mouth began to water.

"I hope you don't mind if I do!" exclaimed Lir. "Although I'm happy to share," he added generously.

"Yes please," said Merryn.

"Me too," added Rohan.

Nixter and Lir beamed and Merryn felt a bit dizzy. Then she shook it off. It was time for business.

"I hope you don't mind me asking but how did my great-aunt come to have a red cap?" she asked.

If Lir was surprised by the suddenness of the question he didn't show it. He began to cut the cake into large pieces.

"I've been asking myself the same thing," he replied.

"Unfortunately the answer is, I don't know. It's not unheard of for humans to obtain a cap. In times past, when our world was closer to yours, caps were sometimes bequeathed to humans and passed down through families. However there's no record of your aunt's cap passing through a family line, until yourself of course. I checked. There were deaths in our world around the time Lorelei began to visit Turrey. I made some enquiries this week, on Nixter's behalf, but the families of the deceased all remember the caps passing over with those who died."

"Did anyone ever ask her?" asked Rohan.

Lir smiled. "That would be considered very rude in our world. One's cap is one's sole responsibility. No one questions or interferes with the keeping and passage of caps."

Nixter looked thoughtfully at Lir. "Do you remember Murgen Merryweather?" he asked.

"I do and I too have followed this line of thinking." Lir looked to his guests. "Murgen was a young merrow. She disappeared with no explanation around the time Lorelei first appeared. No one ever saw her again. But she was a highly spirited individual. Merrow can also live a solitary existence quite happily, especially the females. It is not uncommon for them to take off when they come of age." He shrugged. "It's probably just a coincidence."

Suddenly, the lift door they'd entered through opened. A large weathered looking merrow in uniform, burst into the room.

"Pardon for bargin' in," he announced gruffly.

Lir held up his hand for a moment and interrupted.

"This is Captain Conang, Chief of Merlice. Please continue, Captain."

"Somethin' weird's happenin' out there!" He gestured to the clear glass wall of the circular tower room. "Won't bother explainin'. You can see for yerselves."

Four heads swivelled to gaze to the water beyond the room. Outside, floating in the water, were literally thousands upon thousands of cod fish — very dead-looking fish.

The Autopsy

The herring are not in the tides as they were of old;
— William Butler Yeats, *The Meditation of the Old Fisherman*

"Are they …?" asked Lir, his young face suddenly grave.

"'Fraid so," replied Conang. He walked back to the lift door and beckoned.

A uniformed merrow entered the room. Lying, lifeless in his arms, was a cod. He placed it gently on the ground in front of Lir and retreated. Nixter grabbed his bag and withdrew his medical kit, the one thing, he explained, he never left home without. He removed a stethoscope and placing the two tubular sections inside his ears and the bell-shaped end over the cod's chest, he raised a finger to his lips. He listened in silence for a minute or so. Slowly, he removed the listening device and shook his head.

Turning to face Lir, he spoke. "With your permission, I'd like to transport this cod back to my lab and perform an autopsy. Something here is terribly wrong."

Lir approved immediately. Given the seriousness of the situation he offered to accompany them and with two attendants carrying the cod on a small stretcher, the little entourage set off at once towards Nixter's home.

Nixter took full opportunity of the travelling time to discuss with Conang events leading up to the deaths, en masse, of the fish. Conang took full opportunity to puff on a large cigar. Merryn was bursting to ask how the cigar still smoked underwater … and about the two-inch scar on the Captain's left cheek leading up to an eye-patch, but didn't feel brave enough.

"What happened?" asked Nixter. "We saw the cod gathering on our way to meet with Lir. I remarked at the time that it was unusual to see cod this far south; they usually prefer the colder waters to the north. The next we knew was when you came through the door."

Conang's gruff voice replied. "The cod have bin squirmin' like eels, for some time. Rightly so in my opinion. Bin fished to within an inch of extinction and they're fed up to the gills with it. Intelligence sources to the north wired me there might be some sorta protest, or indignation meetin' as they were calling it — in waters down here — so when I saw 'em gatherin' I called for backup. Seemed peaceful enough. Then, just when numbers peaked, 'bout ten minutes fore I informed you, something strange began to happen. They stopped movin'! Went still for a good bit. Tried shaking a few but they wouldn't respond. Dead as dodos. At the risk of soundin' outta turn, fishy business this."

"I quite agree," said Lir. "And a strange protest. Any ideas Nixter?"

"We can rule out a toxin or poison in the seawater. No one else seems to be affected. It could be a fast-acting virus peculiar to cod, but if it is, it's not one I know. This isn't like any disease I've ever seen. I hate to say it but perhaps the creatures took their own lives. They may have reached a point where it was either the net or themselves. It's a radical move though, and one quite inconsistent with cod psychology. Slow, placid and peace-loving is how I'd describe them."

"Yes," agreed Lir sadly. "Amiable creatures, cod."

Merryn could see that Lir was fond of all sea-life, not just his own kind.

They reached Nixter's house and entered one at a time. Nixter led them through the living room to a well-concealed doorway in the wall, behind a cabinet of shells. He swung the hinged cabinet outward and opened the door.

"This is my lab," he announced and one by one, they stepped into an immaculate and well-equipped surgery.

The stretcher-bearers laid down the stretcher and retreated. Nixter scrubbed his hands thoroughly and swabbed down a steel table. He collected various surgical instruments and placed them carefully on a small trolley. Pulling on a pair of latex gloves, he lifted the cod from its resting place and laid it down onto the steel surface.

"Firstly," Nixter explained in teacher-like tones, "an autopsy is conducted to determine the cause, manner and mechanism of death."

Conang began to yawn loudly but Nixter continued undeterred.

"There are four distinct manners of death: natural, accidental, suicidal and homicidal. Due to the vast numbers of the dead, accidental death is highly unlikely. To determine the cause and mechanism of death, we shall examine the body. Captain Conang! PLEASE put that away. This is a sterile environment."

Conang sheepishly placed the cigar he was unwrapping back in his pocket and sighed heavily. He clearly wasn't one for boring procedure.

"I shall begin by searching for trace evidence."

"What's trace evidence?" asked Rohan.

Nixter looked delighted. "It's trace evidence that frequently leads to a murderer," he replied dramatically. "Hair, clothing fibres, sand, seaweed, any foreign substance that attaches itself to the victim's body, is considered trace evidence. In this case, I'm looking primarily for evidence of poisoning — any strange odours or residue around the mouth could indicate this."

Conang began to tap the underside of the table with his fingertips. "No more questions," he muttered.

Nixter examined around the mouth of the cod and bringing

his nose down, he inhaled strongly. His face remained expressionless. Using a magnifying glass, he examined the body of the fish thoroughly, taking his time to look under every scale.

"No evidence of oral administration or puncture marks, although this means nothing. Many poisons leave no trace."

Conang was now staring up at a point on the ceiling. Merryn had a sneaky suspicion he was indulging in a few eye rolls without being too obvious.

"Let's hope an internal examination will reveal more." Nixter picked up a scalpel and held it directly above the cod.

"I'll begin with a 'y'-shaped incision; a deep cut across the line of the gills, and down the centre of the body. For those who are gutless … err, squeamish, please look away."

Merryn had gutted many fish in her time and felt sure she could cope. Standing alongside Rohan, she continued to observe. Nixter held the scalpel blade above the right gill and brought it down steadily in one movement. He was a millimetre from the surface of the cod when he stopped abruptly and placed the scalpel back on the table. Reaching for his stethoscope, he attached it with speed and rested it over the cod's chest for the second time that day. Conang made to speak but Nixter held up his hand for silence. He listened carefully for a minute or two before removing the earpieces.

"This cod is not dead. It's very nearly dead, but not quite. The correct term for its present condition would be a state of suspended animation. In other words this fish has been zombified!"

"Zombified!" spat Conang. "Your havin' me on!"

"This case gets more and more curious!" exclaimed Lir.

Nixter continued. "There are a couple of natural toxins that could cause this state, but the one I'm thinking of comes from another fish; from the internal organs of the female puffer fish. The active toxin is called *tetradotoxin,* and it can be extracted and made into a substance commonly know as Zombie Powder."

"I've read about that stuff before," said Merryn. "Japanese sushi chefs in our world prepare puffer fish for eating. They leave some of the toxin behind. I think it's called *fugu*. It's supposed to give the eater a tingly feeling. The chefs get it wrong sometimes and people can die."

Merryn stared around at Nixter, Lir and Conang. All three had gone extremely pale. Lir began to apologise.

"Sorry," he said. "It's just the thought of eating fish leaves we merrow feeling a bit queasy. To us, it's cannibalism."

As Merryn nodded sympathetically, Nixter cleared his throat.

"Zombie Powder in the correct dose will cause muscle paralysis, shallow breathing and a heartbeat that is so slow and weak, it's barely detectable. The victim will appear dead and indeed, is very close to death. Sometimes bad side-effects occur when not enough oxygen can be taken in. The most serious of these is brain damage. We need to arrange for the cod to be taken to a holding tank where we can oxygenate the water — as quickly as possible. The zombie powder should wear off in about two to three days."

"We could use the Basin," offered Lir. He looked at Merryn and Rohan. "The Basin is a large crater to the rear of Turrey Palace."

"I'll sort it," said Conang. "If every merrow in Turrey can locate at least fifty cod each and bring 'em to the Basin, we'll have it done in no time. Salty, my second in command, can handle the details."

Conang stepped outside with a message for the stretcher attendants to convey back to Turrey.

Nixter wheeled over a cylinder and placed a tubular end near the cod's gills. "This little fellow should be fine now. He's very fortunate. It was a near thing with that scalpel. I'm beginning to believe that the cod deliberately administered the toxin to themselves. They obviously wanted everyone to believe they were dead."

"Why?" asked Merryn.

"I can think of a good reason," said Lir. "I recently heard a rumour that fishermen are chasing the cod further south. They have all but fished them from their home waters. But, if the fishermen thought that something was wrong with the cod, that they were diseased or had been poisoned, they may seek out new fishing grounds or fish for a different species. Selling unhealthy or toxic fish would put them out of business pretty quickly."

"Cod are delightful fish but not the brightest," said Nixter. "This is a strange protest and one that has a sharp mind behind it. Extracting the toxin and arranging for the cod to self-administer it in the correct dose, requires considerable skill and organisation."

Nixter looked at Conang, who had returned to the room.

"There is someone I can think of who might be capable of masterminding such a stunt ... and pulling it off."

"I'm catchin' yer drift boffin boy," said Conang. "Sturgis Pike!"

Lir nodded.

"Who's Sturgis Pike?" asked Rohan.

Lir answered. "Sturgis Pike is a merrow. He's a great supporter of all sea-life and campaigns strongly for sea animal rights. His heart is in the right place; it's just that some of his methods can be a little extreme. In the last few decades, he's been working closely with whales.

"Some time ago, Sturgis took drastic steps to raise awareness of whales amongst humans. Unfortunately, his campaign also involved great sacrifice. Nearly every year, somewhere in the world, a group of whales beach themselves in protest. Many die in the process, but interest in the human world has led to a more sympathetic understanding of whales."

Conang looked at them impatiently. "This one has Sturgis Pike's fishy fingers all over it. He doesn't live far, just below the Submarine Tavern. I'm gonna pay him a visit. Who's comin'?"

The small group departed immediately with Merryn and Rohan following at the rear. They headed west to Ben-Varrey Bay before taking a downward turn. After swimming a few metres they reached what Merryn thought must be the tavern Conang had referred to. It was made from the hull of an old

wartime submarine and was a cosy-looking retreat with tiny
portholes and a bright coat of emerald paint that helped it to
blend with its surroundings. She peeped through a porthole to
catch a glimpse of the inside. She spied a group of merry
merrow who in turn spotted her. They held up foaming mugs
in a cheerful salute.

Swimming further down, the group eventually reached an
old shack. It was constructed from irregular-shaped pieces of
driftwood, lashed together with coarse rope. Merryn watched
as Conang swam to the front door which was painted a bright
shade of duck egg green. As he gave it a sharp rap she crept
closer and put an ear to the door. Inside, she could hear some
faint scrabbling sounds, then silence. Conang knocked again,
this time harder.

"Open up Sturgis, we know yer in there!"

The door opened a tiny crack. A bright green eye and part
of a pierced snout peered out.

"Sturgis, just be wanting a quick word. It's about the cod."

"I didn't do it," blurted the merrow.

"Do what?" said Conang pushing the door wide. "Did I say
anythin' had bin done?" Nixter slipped past Sturgis and inside.

"Hey, you can't barge in here. I've got rights and I know
'em. Where's yer warrant for starters?"

"Here," said Conang, thrusting a piece of paper at him and
pushing past.

"Hey, this is a cigar wrapper," shouted Sturgis.

"Really?" Conang swam back to the entrance. He snatched
the paper back, pulled out a pen and wrote SEARCH

WARRANT in capitals before signing below. He thrust it back at Sturgis and swam past again.

Sturgis looked outraged. "This isn't valid! It doesn't have the official signature."

A voice spoke from behind.

"Perhaps I could authorise it."

Sturgis looked down to see the young face of his king. He hung his head.

"I was only trying to help 'em. I … I like cod. I feel sorry for 'em."

"Over here," sounded Nixter from the rear of the shack.

Merryn joined the rest of the party in following a length of hallway leading to the back of the house. She saw Nixter standing in a doorway and joined him.

She peered inside. "Wow!"

"Holy sea spray!" spluttered Conang.

"You have been busy," said Lir, arriving with a shame-faced Sturgis.

In front of them, lining every inch of wall space were heated glass aquariums. Behind the panes, swimming happily, were countless puffer fish.

A door at the rear of the aquarium room opened and a loud voice, clearly unaware of visitors, shouted through.

"Hey dude. The fishing boats have gone … oops. Sorry didn't know you had company."

"It's cool Kipper," said Sturgis. "They know." Sturgis looked at Lir and Conang. "This is Kipper. He's been helping distribute the zombie powder."

"We're not in serious trouble, are we?" asked Kipper.

Much like his friend Sturgis, Kipper was a young, whippet-thin merrow. He had long unkempt hair and his t-shirt, tie-dyed in a mass of lurid colour, read in bold letters, 'Cuddle a Cod!' Sturgis sported a similar one which said, 'Hail the Whale!'

Kipper continued with his defence. "It worked — our plan. It was daring but it worked. The fishing boats have headed to new grounds, further north. I heard the fishermen radioing each other. They were freaked out by the um, *dead cod.* They threw their catch back 'n' split the scene."

Sturgis leapt up and punched the air. Then he looked at Lir again and his hand dropped. "Beg yer pardon sir. Are we in trouble?"

Lir suddenly looked every inch Turrey's leader.

"Your motives are not bad," he said sternly, "and as such are hard to punish. It's your methods that are extreme and foolish. You have placed the lives of these cod in grave danger. Thanks to Dr Havmand, we have been able to act quickly and do as much as we can to ensure their well-being, until the toxin wears off. But there may be some cod who'll never be quite the same again. Salty and the residents of Turrey are out in open sea as I speak, trying to locate all of the cod and place them out of harm's way."

"Excuse me, sir," Sturgis interrupted. "I mean no disrespect, but the cod were already in danger. They came to us, not the other way round. We couldn't just ignore 'em."

"Err, did you just say the cod approached you?" interrupted

Nixter. He looked puzzled. "Are you sure you didn't give them just a little help with the idea? As I've said before, cod are placid and peace-loving, but not overly bright. The thought of them taking a stand of their own doesn't fit."

"Honestly, it's the truth sir. We've admitted to drugging the cod, why would we hide anything else? The cod came to me about a month ago with some queer story about seeing a vision. According to a group of the elders, an old woman had appeared before them. The Wizened One, they called her." Merryn saw a puzzled look exchange briefly between Nixter and Lir.

Sturgis continued. "*You must seek the pike,* was all she said before disappearing upwards." Sturgis rolled his eyes. "Apparently, the vision appeared over three nights. Being cod, they took the message literally and thought they were being told to go live with pike who, as we all know, are fresh-water fish. Some poor cod actually tried swimming up an estuary only to die when the water changed. Then one of the brighter ones suggested seeking the Sturgis Pike. It's a strange story but it's the one they told me."

"I don't suppose you remember anything out of the ordinary happening about a month ago?" asked Nixter. "Were you approached in any way?"

"You don't actually believe all that stuff … about seeing a vision?" Sturgis looked surprised. "Cod are superstitious, not to mention gloomy."

"So are most when their numbers are threatened," replied Nixter. "How did you get the puffer fish? They're not local to these waters."

"They just appeared, on the doorstep, err ... about a month ago ... just after the cod approached me. Attached to one of the boxes was an article about the properties of zombie powder. I got the idea straight away." Sturgis paused. "You think I've been manipulated don't you?"

I don't suppose you happened to see who delivered the fish?"

"I heard the knock but when I answered, no one was there, just the fish. Hundreds of 'em, in little bags of warm water, boxed up in fishing crates. I was so busy bringing 'em in and housing 'em, I didn't give their delivery another thought. I'm often lumbered with unwanted pets and wildlife. Everyone knows I'm a sucker for 'em."

"If this is a stunt of some sort, why, and to what purpose?" asked Lir.

"As far as we know the cod will mostly recover and the outcome may even benefit them."

"Excuse me sir," interrupted Kipper. "It's just a thought, but while we're all here, I mean ... the king of Turrey and Nixter and the Captain ... and everyone is out looking for cod ... who's looking after Turrey?"

… most search in vain

Precious Pearls

The sea hath its pearls,
The heaven hath its stars;

—Heinrich Heine, *The Sea Hath Its Pearls*

Nixter spun around. "A colossal diversion! It's more than possible. I've got a bad feeling about this. Turrey and all who inhabit her may be vulnerable."

Suddenly, Merryn felt herself being pulled along the hallway, through Sturgis Pike's front door and into a trail of bubbles left behind by Lir and Conang.

"I must get you back to the bay then on to Turrey." Nixter breathed heavily. Merryn resisted his pull.

"We're coming with you." She made eye contact with Rohan and he nodded.

Nixter looked pale. His usual calm had vanished.

"Please, don't argue, I've not the time. I'm sorry I ever thought to involve you. Don't delay me."

"What are you frightened of?" asked Merryn. "What could happen to Turrey?" Merryn resisted his pulls again until the struggling stopped. She had Nixter's attention. He paused for a moment scratching the side of his head.

"Well … I'm growing more certain that someone or something wants a red cap … wants it badly enough to kill … even an infant. I apologise if we're all a bit jumpy but with the baby incident so recent and now the cod … and Lorelei's death and the curfew … things in and around Turrey feel peculiar — unpredictable — unsafe."

"Are there many mer-babies in Turrey?" asked Rohan.

Nixter's breathing deepened then he slapped his forehead. "Merling House! Lir and Conang will be securing Turrey. The House lies outside its walls."

Nixter swam ahead, his powerful tail tearing seams through the great body of water. Merryn and Rohan struggled to keep up with him. As he neared the Black Hole, he paused to wait for them, his tail flickering impatiently like a cat's.

"Merling House lies just below this reef of coral that surrounds us. Wait here. If I don't return in five minutes you must swim to Turrey for assistance. Don't follow me."

The silver tail sliced the water and Nixter disappeared before they could protest.

With Nixter gone, Merryn felt strangely alone and vulnerable. She swam close to Rohan's side and together they waited in silence. Suddenly, something moved behind them.

They turned at the same time to see an enormous grey fish. Its mouth lay slack and open and on seeing the rows of razor sharp teeth, Merryn realised she'd been mistaken. It wasn't a fish, it was a shark. But it posed no threat to them. A great gash in its side had bled the life force from it. Above them moved a dark shadow. They looked quickly up to see another of the lifeless grey shapes passing by, a dark-red trickle spilling from its flank. The water surrounding them seemed unnaturally still. Here, in this small sheltered body of reef, swam no fish.

"No sign of Nixter," said Rohan. "I'm worried. I know he told us not to but ..."

"I think we should." Merryn ducked swiftly under the lip of coral and rock. Rohan followed quickly behind her. Below them, nestled into the side of the reef, was a tiny dwelling made from the very materials of its setting. This served as a camouflage of sorts and if Nixter hadn't led them practically to the front door they would have easily passed Merling House without ever noticing it. Indeed, on their first trip to Turrey earlier that day, they'd done just that.

Cautiously, Merryn led the way to the building's entrance. Inside a coral portico that framed the front door, an alarming sight met their eyes. It was a merman, a green soldier. He bobbed in the water, a harpoon jutting from his powerful tail. As they ventured closer his eyes flashed open. A look of profound fear came into them. It disappeared as he focused.

"Help me," he pleaded weakly. "Please, pull it out." Merryn

swam up to him and placed a hand on his pale-green shoulder.

"Of course we'll help."

The merman's breath came in shallow gasps. "Don't be afraid, merrow flesh heals quickly. I can't do it myself."

Merryn spoke softly to Rohan. "If you can pull the harpoon, I'll bind the wound."

As she slipped out of her cardigan, Rohan thrust his hand into a small pocket at the side of his rucksack and pulled out a pencil. He placed it between the merman's lips.

"Bite down," he commanded. Merryn watched as Rohan grabbed the shaft of the harpoon and pulled swiftly and firmly. Despite his small frame he was surprisingly strong. He paused momentarily to gather strength. She flinched at the sound of tearing flesh. Rohan grunted and the merman's eyes closed. The pencil snapped in two as the shaft of the harpoon was wrenched free. Merryn wound her garment around the wound, securing it tightly. The merman was still for a moment before, unexpectedly, he opened his eyes again and smiled broadly.

"My name is Aquilis. I'm a guard. Well done my friends. The relief is enormous. I need to rest now, the flesh is already knitting. You must help Nixter, he's in the ward. The intruder has fled, you're in no danger."

Rohan pushed against a metal grill that led from the entrance to the main body of the building. Cautiously they moved forward and inside. The room seemed empty apart from three enormous clam shells. Merryn spotted Nixter. He was kneeling on the floor of the room next to one of the great shells. Alongside him lay a young merrow. Her long gold hair fanned out behind her, contrasting with the blood that flowed freely from a large gash on her forehead. They watched as Nixter removed a length of bandage from his medical kit and bound it carefully around the merrow's head, staunching the flow. Finally he spoke.

"Assistants! I see you obeyed my instructions ... not. But I'm glad to see you. Our timing was fortunate. Our thief was forced to the surface some minutes ago and thanks to Aurelia here, without a cap. The guard is wounded. We must help ..."

"Rohan pulled the harpoon and I bound the wound. He's resting now," said Merryn.

Nixter sat upright, his eyebrows raised. "You two are proving most surprising."

Merryn looked around her. "The babies, where are they?"

Nixter opened his medical bag removing a small brown bottle labelled *Restorative*. "I think you need to know a little about mer-babies," he said, pouring a little of the golden liquid into a cup. He held it against Aurelia's pale lips. She didn't wake but her breathing deepened.

"Mer-babies grow inside the shell of a *Tridacna gigus,* these giant clams you see here."

"You mean there are babies, inside these?" Merryn gasped. "Never! How did they get there? Why so few? Only three ..."

Nixter smiled for the first time since they'd entered.

"One question at a time. Firstly, a mer-couple who want a baby must find the pearl from an oyster-like bivalve, before implanting it in one of these shells." Nixter's smile faded and he looked suddenly very sad.

"Natural pearls are extremely rare. Waters around the world are becoming more polluted, and bivalves are sensitive creatures. They are unhappy in dirty or toxic water. They don't thrive. Over the last few centuries, your pearl divers have taken most of the naturally formed pearls. Only a few lucky and well-concealed ones remain. Merrow travel thousands of miles to seek them and, sadly, most search in vain. We used to have large families but now, only a fortunate few manage even one child. Mer-babies have become terribly precious."

"How do the babies get the red caps?" asked Rohan.

"Before sealing the pearl inside the clam, two things are added: the egg of a robin and the egg of a money spider. Once the clam is sealed, the eggs hatch and the pearl transforms. The robin sheds its breast feathers and the money spider weaves them magically into the *cohuleen druith*. It's because these two creatures derive from the earth that the cap has such special properties that allow merrow to survive in either realm."

"Did someone try to open the shell?"

Another voice answered for Nixter. It was surprisingly strong and the tone clear and melodious.

"She tried, but luckily for this baby her mother had her wits about her."

Aurelia had wakened. She sat up and put a hand to her head, looking from Nixter to the two children.

"Few can open a clam. Once sealed, it's protected by powerful magic. It can only be opened by a secret word or phrase, a *passage* known to the mother alone. Sometimes the grandmother is told — in case something happens to the mother. It's no good threatening or torturing either of them for a passage. I don't know what mothers and grandmothers are like in your world, but in ours, they are ferociously protective. We would happily die protecting our babies. No merrow has ever revealed a passage; it wouldn't happen.

"Please, could I have another drop of your wonderful medicine Dr Havmand?"

Nixter held the bottle to her lips. She took a generous mouthful and paused to swallow before introducing herself to Merryn and Rohan.

"My name is Aurelia Aquabelle." She stroked the rough surface of the great shell by her side. "My baby is in here."

"What happened today?" asked Nixter. "How did someone get past the sharks. Their senses are totally accurate. Only mothers and merlitia can hope to pass inside. Those who are not, Neptune help them!"

"I invited her. She tricked me. I thought her to be my mother."

"But your mother …"

"Died, I know, in the terrible storm of '52." Aurelia lowered her head sadly. "Too early in my childhood to fully remember her."

She turned to Merryn and Rohan.

"She disappeared in wild waters while trying to secure our home. Her body was never found. You can imagine my state of mind earlier today when an older merrow appeared before me, and announced who she was. She explained her absence of many years saying she'd taken advantage of the fierce currents the storm created to search the ends of the earth for something precious for her beloved daughter, me. She held out her hand to reveal a pearl.

"The thought of having back my mother and the prospect of not one but two children was almost too much for me. The strangest part was that my 'mother' did not have a red cap." Aurelia paused and Merryn heard Nixter's sudden sharp intake of breath.

"She begged me to take her to the shell in which her grandchild lay," continued Aurelia. "I felt overwhelmed ... and sorry for her. I led her here. She was my guest and the sharks paid us no heed. When we arrived and she saw the shell, she pleaded with me for the passage, so that she could feel like a proper grandmother. I acted foolishly but she had a glamour about her ... and she looked strangely familiar. I was mesmerised — could barely resist. However, I gave a false passage. It was a test to see how she would react if the shell didn't open. I remember enough of my real mother to know what her reaction would have been. She'd have suffered immense disappointment and asked at once if she'd misunderstood. When the shell did not open the imposter forced me to the ground and began to torture me." Aurelia shuddered. "I remember her face, so cruel. It was turning blue just before I passed out."

"She may have been drowning," said Nixter. "You were fortunate she was forced to the surface so urgently. On her way out, she shot Aquilis with his own harpoon. He'll survive thanks to our two friends here. She killed a couple of the sharks before they could do the same to her."

Lir and Conang led by Aquilis, burst into the room. Lir's young face was flushed and he gulped deep breaths before attempting to speak.

"We came, as soon as we could. Turrey was as we left it. We guessed, too late, it was here the danger lay."

"The thief left without a cap," said Nixter looking from the top of Merryn's head to the great shell by Aurelia's side. "Aurelia and Aquilis shall recover but I'm afraid we've lost our ultimate soldiers. She has killed two and the rest have gone. Sharks are loyal only to themselves. They assist us for the opportunity of a kill. They lost five of their group during the first break-in. I'm not sure they'll be coaxed back now."

Merryn took her eyes from Aurelia's shell for a moment to listen as Lir spoke to the guard.

"Aquilis, what did you see? Was it human or merrow?"

Aquilis hesitated seeming uncertain of what he was about to say next.

"This may sound strange," he said eventually. "I've never seen one but, she looked like something my grandmother used talk about when I was a young merrow. It usually came up when she was lecturing me on the importance of keeping my cap safe. Her aim was to frighten me into being more responsible. She used to tell stories, awful scary stories about …" Aquilis swayed a little and looked down at the seabed. "The thief, she reminded me of a … sea wraith."

The room was silent. Merryn looked around at the faces. Even Lir's was deathly pale. "Wh ... what's a sea wraith?" she eventually asked.

It was some time before Nixter answered. He took a deep breath. "A sea wraith is a merrow ... to which something unimaginably awful has happened. I can't think of a human equivalent ... perhaps being buried alive. A sea wraith is a merrow who no longer has a cap. Instances are rare and can be catastrophic. Certainly it's never happened in our community, at least not in my lifetime." He looked down. "The one who loses the cap can never return to the water, yet they will not be human enough for your world. It's a living hell. Wracked with constant pain and forced to live in swamps or underground they usually die a slow and torturous death." Nixter turned away from them.

Merryn saw tears streaming from Aurelia's eyes.

Lir spoke next. "Although our hearts break for the wraith and what they have lost and must endure, they are also to be feared. I've heard stories of sea wraiths from my ancestors, so far back in time that no one quite knows whether they're myth or truth. I've heard that sea wraiths with strong desires and inner reserves of strength can tap into dark forces. They will find a way to return to their former communities and destroy them. They are feared for these reasons."

"Wh ... what do you mean by dark forces?" asked Merryn.

"Just like people, there are many types of faerie creatures. Not all are good. Some are mischievous, some are naughty and some are downright evil. They use whatever power they possess to trick or convey bad luck. The one positive thing is that usually these spirits work alone and, with the odd exception, rarely become too powerful. A sea wraith wallows in pain and misery. If they live long enough for bitterness to grow from this, the wraith will be attracted to these beings like a magnet. The clever wraith will learn from them. The wraith with any force of personality will eventually command these creatures."

Nixter turned to them again and took another deep breath. "We came across a loireag last week. She was residing in seawater near an unexplored passage entrance. I think she was guarding it."

Before Lir could reply, Aurelia interrupted. She clutched Nixter's sleeve, her knuckles white.

"I've remembered! I thought she looked familiar. She wasn't my mother, she was once my friend. The sea wraith was Murgen Merryweather. I'm sure of it."

Firewood and Fur

"She lifted up her head and stretched her arms to the sea,
She was changed to a seal as I watched from afar:
Dividing the waves, O strongly went she
To the boundless spaces where her kindred are."

— Manx Gaelic Folksong, *Lament of the Sealwoman's Lover*

The small room in Merling House was silent. All eyes focused on Aurelia. Water rippled and swirled echoing the thoughts that filtered through Merryn's head. *She disappeared then Auntie had a cap! Auntie wasn't a thief ...*

"Do you think my aunt stole Murgen's cap?" Merryn blurted out. She felt her cheeks redden.

Lir stared at her. "No!" he exclaimed. "Over the years, Turrey came to know your aunt well. She respected our world deeply and because of that she was always a welcome visitor. I don't think she stole the cap but it does seem likely now that your cap once belonged to Murgen. How Lorelei came to have it is anyone's guess. Perhaps it's not important."

Not to you, thought Merryn. *It's mine now. I need to know.*

"We have a sea wraith in our midst. If she succeeds in replacing her cap, we could all be in great danger. But enough said. It's been a long day and you have both been brave. The Captain shall escourt you home. We will close Merling House and move these precious shells to Turrey." Lir gazed at the remaining clams, his eyes filling with a deeper sadness. "This building is no longer necessary."

"Indeed," said Nixter. "I'll stay to assist our patients. He turned to Merryn and Rohan. "Visit me, as soon as you can. We have much to talk about and some ideas are starting to form." He took Merryn's hand in his. "Don't fret. We'll get to the bottom of this."

Later, as Merryn arrived home and entered the kitchen, she found her mother, of all things, was crumbing some fillets of fish.

"I hope you're not using cod," she blurted out.

"Don't be silly," replied Mrs O'Reilly in her usual brisk manner. "I never buy cod if I can help it. I'm using a distant cousin of the cod called pollock. It's cheaper and there's more of it."

The following Friday in the canteen, Merryn was packing her lunch box back into her bag anticipating the bell.

"What time shall we meet tomorrow?" asked Rohan.

"Is ten o'clock okay? At the bay?"

"Err … Merryn?"

She looked up.

"Would you like to come to my house first … for breakfast? You can meet my dad."

"Sure. I'd like that." Merryn felt a jolt of surprise but tried not to show it.

At half-past eight the following morning, she raced across the headland to the Cringles' farm. On reaching the small cottage facing the sea, she knocked heartily on the door. A tall man with untidy blonde hair and piercing blue eyes opened up.

"Hello! I'm Joe Kelly, call me Joey. You must be Merryn. Come in, Rohan's expecting you."

Merryn stepped inside. The house was small and sparsely furnished but it smelt delicious. Mr Kelly led her through to a tiny makeshift kitchen where Rohan was standing in front of a portable gas cooker. He turned around.

"Hey, glad you could make it. You met Dad?"

"Yeah." She smiled at Mr Kelly. "Something smells good," she added.

"Scrambled egg sandwiches okay?" asked Rohan.

"Sounds great, I'm starving."

Rohan finished assembling the first one and wrapping it in foil, he handed it to his dad.

"Can't stick around I'm afraid," said Mr Kelly. "Got to work today. Nice meeting you. See you again sometime." He ruffled Rohan's hair and made his way out of the room. The front door slammed.

"I thought we could eat upstairs, in my room," said Rohan.

Merryn stood next to him and watched as he buttered four slices of brown bread. He spooned scrambled egg over two slices before slapping down a top layer of bread. He placed the finished sandwiches onto two plates and tore off strips of kitchen roll before handing a plate to her.

"Follow me," he said.

She trotted after him to the back of the kitchen. Holding her plate high, she followed him in climbing up a rickety loft ladder. When she reached the top, she placed her plate at the side of a small opening and climbed though. Rohan was sitting on a camp bed stretched alongside a window munching away. She spotted a wicker chair in the corner and picking up her plate, she walked over to it and sat down.

They ate in silence enjoying their food. Merryn swallowed her last mouthful and wiped her hands on a piece of the kitchen roll.

"I like your room," she said. "Cool view." Putting her plate down on the floor she walked to the loft window and gazed across to Ben-Varrey Bay. The tide was out and a small dog raced across the sand chasing a ball.

"I like being close to the sea," said Rohan. "It reminds me of Mum. We used to live across there."

Merryn followed the line of his finger to the faint length of mainland visible on the horizon. She held her breath.

"Mum disappeared over there, when I was five. I saw her go. Our old house was by the sea. My bed used to lie against a window, just like this one. I could see the water at night. Sometimes magic silver balls would come across with the waves. I liked to watch them." Rohan looked up at Merryn's puzzled expression but he didn't laugh. He looked down again. "That's what I thought they were. They used to bob and float and disappear, then surface again … like magic! One night, while I was watching the balls, Mum went outside. I saw her. She walked into the water and followed them out to sea. The moon came out then and I knew what the balls were. They were heads, the silver heads of seals." He turned his gaze back to the window. "I never saw her again. I didn't know it at the time but, she'd left something behind — something she couldn't survive without."

Merryn didn't know what to say. Rohan's hands had been clenched the whole time he'd been speaking. She knew that what he was telling her was painful for him.

"Do you want to see a photo of her?" he asked suddenly.

"I'd like that." Merryn watched as he reached under his bed and pulled out a small box.

"Wow, the box, is beautiful!" she exclaimed.

"Thanks. Dad made it for me. It's a puzzle box." He handed it to her. "Try and open it?"

Merryn took the box with both hands and turned it over, then over again. She stroked the smooth darkly polished wood and rubbed her thumbs across its edges. There was no opening she could see, no seams.

"How …?"

Rohan stretched out an arm and reluctantly, she handed the box back. She watched as he pressed a tiny section at its base. A side flap sprung open.

"How did you do that?"

"Magic!"

Rohan reached inside and pulled out a photo. It's corners were bent and he tried to smooth them out before handing it to her. She took it from him.

"Mum's name was Nuala."

Merryn looked down at the photo. Sitting on a strip of beach, was a young woman. Her face was turned to one side and she gazed behind almost longingly. Sleek fair hair was braided into a long plait that reached to her waist.

"She's beautiful. You look just like her."

Rohan reached inside the puzzle box again. He pulled out a piece of paper.

"She used to sing this to me."

Merryn took the paper from him and stared at the faint black script. She tried to read it but it made no sense.

"It's another language. Mum knew it. It used to be spoken in these parts a long time ago. The song's a story really." Rohan paused to take a deep breath. "It's about a merrow and a fairy creature called a selkie. The selkie can take the form of a human on land and a seal in the water. Do you want to hear it?"

Merryn nodded.

"One day a selkie was swimming. A fisherman caught it and

skinned it for its fur. He thought it was dead and threw it back into the water. The selkie was cold and miserable. It sank down to the ocean floor and drifted into the cave of a merrow. The merrow was kind and took pity on the selkie. She came up with a dangerous plan to get the fur back. She allowed the fisherman to catch her. Then she saw the fur at the bottom of his boat, but before she could get to it and return to the water, the fisherman tied her hands behind her back. This stopped her from being able to remove a special thing she wore, a *cohuleen druith*, which would allow her to breathe the outside air. Once she was out of the water and couldn't breathe, she died. Her death released a terrible storm that capsized the boat and drowned the fisherman. The skin drifted down to the seabed and into the cave just in time to save the selkie."

Merryn turned from the window and looked at Rohan. "I know what you are," she said.

"I'm glad. I'm sorry I couldn't tell you." He looked shy. "I'd err, like to think we're friends."

"We're best friends. Wanna go swimming?"

"Too right!"

Giving Rohan just enough time to place the photo and paper back into their protective box and put it away, Merryn took the lead. Grabbing their plates in one hand she clambered down the loft ladder. Passing through the kitchen, she dumped the plates into the sink and raced outside to the fresh air. Rohan shut the door and was behind her. They were halfway across the headland before he stopped suddenly and shouted out.

"I've forgotten my rucksack — won't be doing much swimming. Race you back."

Reaching the front door of his house first, Merryn leaned against the side wall panting. Rohan reached the door seconds later. He pulled it open then hesitated. She saw a jolt of fear cross his face. She leaned forward to see Rohan's dad blocking the entrance. In his right hand was a thermos, in his left hand was the rucksack.

"Forgot my coffee. You forgotten something, Son?"

Merryn saw the look that exchanged between them. She knew in a heartbeat Rohan's dad had found the seal skin ... and that he knew what it was. She stood silent, not daring to speak.

"Well take it — you'll not be having much fun without it!"

Nervously, Rohan reached out and grasped the bag. He went to pull it to him but his dad held firm.

"I've known for a while. I'll not be taking it from you. I made that mistake once before and it cost me dearly. I trust you, Son."

He released the pack into Rohan's grasp.

Rohan looked into his father's eyes.

"I'll be really careful Dad. I won't let you down and I'll always come home."

Merryn's heart was pounding as they said goodbye and sprinted back across the open expanse. They reached the top of the cobbled path and together followed it down to the sea. Snowflakes swirled around them, melting in the salty air before they could land. Two children and a small dog were playing on the beach. Merryn and Rohan stood back, waiting for them to depart.

"Did your fur once belong to your mum?" asked Merryn.

"Yes. Dad hid it from her. I think he was frightened she would return to the sea and never come back. She missed her sea family too much in the end and returned without it."

Rohan's eyes looked more liquid than normal and Merryn pretended to stare at the small wave breaking on the shore.

"Where did you find her fur?"

"Inside a puzzle box — a big one. It was in with the firewood. Dad used to tell me never to use the wood from the bottom of the pile. One day he wasn't home. It was cold and I used all the wood. A big log looked different from the rest. I knew at once it was a puzzle box. I put it aside then hid it in my room. It was a tricky box — took me a while to open. Then I found the fur. Something inside me knew what it was. It's hard to explain but I just knew. One night, not long after we moved here, I sneaked out and went swimming. You know the rest."

"Was your dad mad when he saw the wood gone?"

"No, he just seemed really sad for a while. He never mentioned it. I didn't know he knew I'd taken it. But I'm glad now."

They waited for the beach to clear then entered the water. Merryn closed her eyes and let the warmth envelop her. She spiralled downwards lost in the sensation of water rippling through her hair, her fingers, across her face. They were approaching Nixter's house when Rohan began to slow down.

Suddenly, he reached out and pulled her back, breaking her trance.

"What's wrong? Why have we stopped?"

"Something doesn't feel right. Look around."

Merryn gazed about. The water was still. She could see no signs of life — no fish — no anemones swaying. Suddenly, she felt cold and her stomach knotted. Before she could speak a long flash of blue began to streak towards her. She tensed her body ready for an impact. Then, a split-second before contact, the blue streak turned abruptly and made for the surface at an unnatural speed.

"What was it?" cried Rohan.

"I don't know. For a second I thought it was a torpedo. Let's hurry. We'll ask Nixter."

As they swam on, fish appeared from rock crevices and seaweed clumps, coral clusters and holes in the seabed. They began to dart about, breathing life back into the water. By the time they'd reached Nixter's, all seemed normal again. Merryn put her hand out to knock. A shout of 'come in' greeted them. She followed Rohan into Nixter's front room waving to Nixter who was busy in the kitchen. The kettle was on and a large plate of lime-coloured pies lay on the table.

Merryn looked around. Nixter had rearranged his living room. A cabinet of shells had been moved to the left side of the room and the double doors to his lab were open, making it part of the living space. The sofa and coffee table had been pushed to an empty space closer to the kitchen and in their place he'd positioned a large desk. A cabinet lay to one side and a bookcase to the other. Its shelves were bulging with all manner of text-books. She swam over and glanced at some titles. *Waves of Crime, Even the Sea Leaves Traces* and *Anatomy of the North Atlantic,* lay spine against spine.

"Take a seat," said Nixter. "And help yourselves to a pie or three. I make the fruit mince myself, from sea grapes."

Merryn's mouth began to water. She swam towards the kitchen and sat beside Rohan. Nixter sat down opposite them and they all reached for a pie at the same time. Nixter paused between bites.

"I hate to ruin our tea party talking about a sea wraith but I think it's time for action. The idea to advertise our services in the hope of getting information was good but so far hasn't achieved much. I helped Mrs Greensleeves locate her lost purse last week and received some gossip about one of our sirens and a top Trimetta player, but nothing of consequence. This approach may be more long term than I'd anticipated."

Merryn swallowed her pie in one gulp before interrupting. "Nixter, something strange just happened, outside." Wiping crumbs from her cheek, Merryn described the incident. Nixter put down the remnants of his pie abruptly.

"What do you think it was?"

Nixter's silence and horrified expression answered for her.

"Should we go straight home?" she asked.

"No. You're definitely safer down here for the time being. She was blue because she was dying. A merrow can survive for a short time in water without a cap. Fifteen minutes is about the maximum though. She'll need time to recover.

Lucky you weren't just a few seconds earlier. She must have been waiting and hoping to spot you. It's my fault. I put your names in the advertisement. She knows who you are and where to find you. She's not without spies. She knows you have her cap."

Before Nixter could say more he was interrupted again by a loud knock from the front entrance.

"Dr, er, Detective Havmand!" A merman in crisp uniform swam into the room. He looked about the same age as Nixter and as he leaned against a wall to catch his breath, Nixter introduced him.

"This is Sgt Salty Skipper."

Merryn stared at him. Salty looked so serious. He had finely cropped green hair, thick glasses and an assortment of note pads and pens protruding from his pocket. He saluted them formally before continuing.

"We need your help, urgently, in Turrey."

"What's wrong?" exclaimed Nixter.

"Winter Tide."

"Yes, preparations begin today."

The sergeant shook his head.

"What could stop it?"

"The theft of the decorations ... and the *works*, that's what!"

"They've gone?"

"Gone! As you know, they're stored in a vault below the market square. It's never locked and people are free to drop by year-round and add to the pile. It's unthinkable anyone would take these things. They are dear to the hearts of all merrow. Conang is ranting and scratching his head and Lir is devastated. He loves this night as much as the children."

"We'll come at once!"

Nixter reached to the drawer of his desk and pulled out two tightly packed bags. He handed one to each of his assistants.

"While I gather my things, check with the inventories inside these and make sure you have all of the items."

Merryn and Rohan opened their bags cautiously. With growing curiosity they pulled out the contents. Each contained a magnifying glass, a waterproof digital camera, tweezers, plastic zip-lock bags, superglue, latex gloves, plastic booties and a face-mask.

Sgt Skipper looked on wide-eyed.

They re-packed the bags and clutching them tightly, set off to Turrey behind Nixter and Salty. On the way, Merryn asked the first question.

"What's Winter Tide?" she blurted out.

Sgt Skipper replied. "It's a very important day in the merrow calendar. It falls on the twenty-fifth of December, although most of our celebrating happens on the eve. Lir leads a colourful ceremony. The special fish from his star-gazing pond light up the central courtyard and Turrey is treated to a spectacular bubbleworks display. Our finest sirens sing and distribute presents to all of our young. It's a wonderful night we all share in."

"What are bubbleworks?" asked Rohan.

Sgt Skipper's serious young face lit up.

"They're a sight to behold! Turrey's lucky enough to have

Gilly Greensleeves as one of its residents. He's the finest bubbleologist in the whole underwater world. Using special gases and detonators combined with just a touch of magic, he can create bubble spectaculars that will knock your scales off. Bubbles of all shapes and sizes; bubbles that can explode into kaleidoscopes of colour and form; bubbles that can spin, float or dance to sounds and song ..."

Arriving at the gates of Turrey Palace, Merryn followed behind Sgt Skipper to the scene of the crime. She looked about. The palace square had been cleared and Conang had taped off an area surrounding the storage vault. Together, they greeted Lir who was looking very down-at-tail, although he cheered up when Nixter slipped him a bag of the mince pies.

"Thanks for coming. We've no time to lose. Whoever has made off with our treasures may be getting further away every second. We do know that at eight pm yesterday, the vault was full. Could you please continue Captain? I feel I need consoling." Lir bit deeply into a mince pie.

"All we know is that Melody Warbler swung by with a batch of presents an' decorations yesterday evenin'," said Conang. "Gilly entered a short time later with the works. We haven't heard of anyone else visitin' the vault till nine this mornin' when the decorative committee arrived to start work. They sure gotta shock."

"We all did," mumbled Lir, crumbs flying.

Nixter interrupted. "Has anyone disturbed the scene?"

"Had a quick mooch round first thing," replied Conang.

"Didn't find a scrap. The committee geezers were too gutted … err… upset to enter. Sent for me."

"Good. It's unfortunate but water destroys evidence far more quickly than air. It's especially important not to churn the water unnecessarily. I shall enter the vault alone for the preliminary investigation. Please observe from a distance."

Nixter placed a camera around his neck and encased his hands in latex gloves before picking up his bag. Carefully, he drew back the wooden trapdoor and entered the vault.

Merryn peered down and watched as he pulled out a plastic bag and a pair of tweezers from his bag, and picked up a small item from the sandy floor.

"Ah, appears to be the butt from a Sirena Cigar! Tut-tut, Captain. Your brand I believe? So far, all evidence leads to you. If I were a lesser detective I would be making a quick arrest."

"Yeah yeah boffin boy. Dropped it this mornin', so what?"

"So, *you must take more care not to contaminate a scene!*"

Conang rolled his eyes and Nixter continued his methodical search. He lingered for a short while over a patch of sand just to the left of the centre of the vault. Whatever he was looking at was invisible to Merryn. Eventually, he opened his bag and pulled out a can of spray paint. Aiming about a foot or so above the layer of sand, he sprayed a film of black paint across its surface.

"I can see some unusual prints on the seabed. They may be marks from where the decorations lay but I don't think so. The sand is pale and the prints are hard to see. I'm using this dark paint to create a contrast. Assistant Kelly, I require your steady hands."

Rohan carefully entered the enclosure as Nixter removed a box from his bag. He placed it in Rohan's hands and guided him into place.

"I'm using a technique called interference holography which can sometimes reveal prints in very soft surfaces, such as sand or carpet. The split laser beam inside the box is being directed at the paint to create a holographic image of our print."

Rohan flicked on a switch as directed. Suddenly visible was a wide, smooth print a bit like a tyre mark only it didn't run in a straight line. The indentation was wavy and rippled across the seabed, tapering towards the end.

At Nixter's request Rohan stepped backwards moving the box further away. Another nearly identical thick, wavy line appeared alongside the first. Nixter photographed the indentations carefully. Happy with the results, he disengaged the laser beam and began resurveying the area. Studying the surface of the underside of the trapdoor, he gave a small gasp. Ushering Rohan out of the vault, he pulled on a facemask and from his kit, grabbed a box labelled, litmus papers'.

Merryn knew from science classes at school, that litmus paper was used for testing the acidity or alkalinity of various substances. She watched as Nixter laid some of the special papers over a blotchy, indented patch on the trapdoor. The papers turned a brilliant shade of scarlet. They bubbled and sizzled before vapourising completely.

"Phew, definitely acidic!" announced Nixter.

He continued scanning the surface of the trapdoor, then made to move away. At the last second, he gave a double take.

"Slithering sea slugs!" he cried before pointing out another seemingly invisible find.

"We have here what I believe may be an entire print. Whoever or whatever pushed this door open has left an impression and I intend to capture it. Prints often leave behind an oily residue. They're quite hard to lift in water and don't last long, but I think we may be in time to capture this one. Merryn, pass me your cartridge of cyanoacrylate please."

"Err … the what?"

"Just asking for the superglue. It's a useful agent for lifting prints."

Nixter pulled a stick-like gadget from his bag and reached up to take a small cylinder from Merryn. He inserted the cylinder into the gadget and speaking through his mask, explained the procedure.

"This is called a fuming wand. I've switched the device on and it's heating the cartridge. Keep well back. It will shortly begin to release vapour."

Nixter held the wand for several minutes and waved it back and forth over the area of the print until he was satisfied. After switching it off, he removed from his kit another portable light source, this time an ultraviolet one. He turned it on and held it over the print. A huge neon claw fluoresced before them.

"What in Hades made that?" rasped Conang.

"What has a large worm-like body, two claws and breathes an extremely corrosive variety of poison?"

Conang answered first. "If I didn't know any better and we weren't standin' at the bottom of the ocean, I'd say you were describin' a serpent."

Wet Rope

"There dwells a loved one,
But cruel is she;
She left lonely forever
The kings of the sea."

— Matthew Arnold, *The Forsaken Merman*

"It's a melusine, isn't it?" said Lir.

"Try two," replied Nixter.

Conang reached for a cigar and at the same time, Lir bit broadly into another pie. For a few short minutes silence reigned.

Eventually Merryn had to ask. "Excuse me, but what's a melusine?"

Conang and Lir had their mouths full and Nixter replied.

"They are a type of extremely rare water spirit. They generally dwell on land for one reason; when they touch water their form and nature changes. From beautiful women, they transform into serpents."

"You mean serpents, as in dragons?" exclaimed Rohan.

"Yes. They are a form of dragon, but wingless and nearly impossible to kill. Also, although unable to breathe fire, they are extremely venomous. Their fangs secrete a type of corrosive poison that works like the strongest of acids. It will dissolve anything on contact and I mean anything. Metal, glass, rock — and flesh and bone! They've not been seen in this realm for many centuries. Whoever has lured them here we can only guess."

"The sea wraith," muttered Conang, flicking cigar ash.

"My conclusion precisely, Captain," agreed Nixter.

"How could she lure not one, but two melusines into her employ?" exclaimed Lir. "They bow to no one."

"They have one weakness, a love of gold," replied Nixter. The wraith probably enticed them on this mission to secure their interest. Most of the festival decorations that adorn the square and palace are crafted from gold. Although material wealth matters little to merrow, Turrey has a vast treasury, I'm guessing she has promised the melusines a portion of this — if they assist her.

"Are we gonna try an' get the booty back or what?" demanded Conang.

"I'm just thinking about that," said Nixter. "I doubt the sea wraith had our festival stuff removed in the hope we would follow her. The clues are subtle. I think she wants to let us know she is present and take the opportunity to suck a little happiness out of our lives. Also, I doubt she'll have destroyed anything. The goods won't be far away. I have an idea. With your permission, I'll set off tonight. If she's nearby, she won't be expecting action during our curfew."

Nixter prepared to leave at once. Saying goodbye to Lir and Conang, Merryn and Rohan followed him to Ben-Varrey Bay. Nixter escourted them right up to the beach this time and waited until they had safely exited the water. Merryn watched him swim away and felt a twinge of sadness.

"I don't want him to go alone," she sighed to Rohan. "We're his assistants; we should be assisting."

"He'd never let us, especially not you. If the sea wraith is involved, it could be dangerous."

"But if Nixter crosses her, he'll need some bargaining power. And what about the loireag? How will he get past her?"

"Nixter's smart. He'll have thought it through. We've got to trust him."

Dusk came early and it would soon be dark. After the warmth of the water, the evening air was freezing. The sounds of carol singers carried across with the wind, and Merryn could make out the lights of the Christmas tree glowing in her living room window. She waved goodbye to Rohan and stopped to watch for a moment as he marched further on along the path, his hands deep inside his pockets.

Merryn rolled over and glanced at her bedside clock. It was eleven-thirty. She felt restless and couldn't sleep. She thought about Nixter and the mer-children. No winter festival and no presents to look forward to. She threw off her bedclothes and jumped out of bed. Pulling on some warm clothes and grabbing her cap, she tip-toed out of her room and paused at the top of the stairs. She could hear the sound of the kettle humming in the kitchen below… nearly drowned out by Dad's tuneless humming. *With all that practice you'd think he'd get better.* She shuddered then jumped as Mum's piercing voice swamped the other noises.

"You making cocoa, love? I'll have one."

She waited for a couple of minutes until Dad had walked from the kitchen to the living room holding two steaming mugs. Watching from the dark stairwell, she saw him put the drinks down and walk back to shut the frosted glass doors to the living room. Merryn slipped quietly down the stairs and out of the back door. *I hope they don't check on me before bed. No reason to …*

The freezing night air bit at her nose and eyes making them water as she raced across the headland and down the path to the bay below. A near full moon cast a pale, silvery light over the surrounding rocks and sand. She'd just reached into her pocket for the cap when something grabbed her shoulder from behind. She swung sharply around, her body tensed.

"Rohan! Phew! You frightened me stupid. What are you doing here?"

"What am I doing here? What are you doing here? Didn't mean to scare you, sorry. Didn't want to call out in case someone heard. Couldn't sleep, bit worried about Nixter. Do you think he's all right?"

"Course I am." A voice spoke sharply from behind.

They jumped at the same time and spun around.

"What are you doing here … and out of the water?" exclaimed Merryn.

"I had an idea," said Nixter. He held his cap in his hands and his beautiful eyes gleamed brightly in the moonlight. "I needed to explore it. Sorry for scaring you. You really shouldn't be here. It's dangerous … but I'm glad to see you." Nixter smiled broadly. Merryn felt her knees go weak.

"Maybe you can help," he added. "Remember the night we followed the passage to the blowhole?"

"Who could forget?" replied Merryn.

"That other passage, the one I couldn't remember, I wanted to try to figure out which direction it follows. I've come up here to check out the lie of the land. I've a feeling that the passageway travels directly underneath the cliff path, but where it leads to, I'm not sure."

There was silence for a few moments then Rohan spoke.

"I once heard Mr Cringle, the farmer who owns the property I live on, talk about this area. When he was young, Mr Cringle and some local boys stumbled across underground caves around here. They used to explore them from time to time until a big landslide sealed off the entrance."

"Interesting," replied Nixter. His eyes narrowed and he began to pace. "A wraith can no longer survive for any length of time in seawater, but will want to be close to her old home. An underground coastal cave would make the ultimate lair. The passageway, the one the loireag may be guarding, could well be the underwater entrance to a cave system, with the blowhole as a land entry point. I have a feeling it will be at the end of that passage that we, sorry I, might find our goodies."

"You mean we can't come?" cried Merryn.

"We want to help," pleaded Rohan.

"This could be a most dangerous assignment. To allow you to enter what could be the lair of the sea wraith — it's unthinkable. You're far too valuable to me as assistants … and friends. Who knows what creatures she has doing her bidding. I'm sorry, but it's out of the question."

"Well, I hope you can sing," said Merryn. "There may be an angry loireag to charm."

"And I hope you can manage the stuff on your own," added Rohan. "The poor wee children with no presents …"

"Or bubbleworks …"

"Or pretty decorations …"

Nixter clapped his hands over his ears. He turned his back on them and began to walk to the cliff path. Merryn lowered her head in disappointment. Then she jerked it back up again.

"You'll stay behind me at all times and do everything I ask. If a situation arises where I demand you leave without me, you must do so. Do you solemnly promise?"

"We do!"

Merryn and Rohan ran to Nixter.

"Come along then, before I regret it," said Nixter, sounding like he already did. "It's low tide. We'll enter through the blowhole."

Merryn scrambled back up to the cliff path and followed Nixter to the great hole in the ground. Looking down, she watched him descend using crags and ledges for hand and foot holds. Rohan followed him. She paused for a moment watching the dark water swirling around the base of the hole. Cap in place, she slipped below.

Apart from the sound of water lapping at the side of the tunnel, all was eerily quiet. She'd forgotten just how dark the passage was. The three managed to link hands in the black and began to inch their way forward. After a couple of minutes, Merryn felt the tunnel wall disappear. They'd reached the unexplored passage entrance.

"It's vital we stay together," Nixter whispered. "I have a length of rope with me. I'm going to tie it to my belt. You will hold on to it tightly and follow me. Merryn, place yourself directly behind me. And Rohan, you stay at the rear this time. Hold onto the rope with your right hand and use your left to steady yourselves and feel your way along the passage. Any sign of trouble and you must make your own way back to the blowhole — as fast as you can. Look after yourselves first and foremost. And Merryn, you must protect your cap — at all costs."

Slowly, they found their positions and began to grope their way forward. The water was still and seemed even denser than before. They'd travelled only a couple of metres when Merryn froze. A nasty gnashing sounded in her right ear. Something grabbed her hair and wrenched it painfully hard. Nixter, in front and Rohan, behind, stopped dead still.

"*Toon* or I bites," rasped a familiar voice.

Merryn opened her mouth and tried to form a sound but nothing happened. Fear had locked her throat.

"*Toon ... Toon!*"

She forced herself to relax and this time a note slipped out. Keeping her voice low and steady, she hummed an old hymn she'd known since childhood. Her hair was released and the close presence of the loireag slipped away. She felt Nixter squeeze her arm and still humming softly, they pushed forwards.

Continuing for what seemed an eternity, the tunnel suddenly ended. She groped around feeling nothing but the slippery sides of the passage and a definite walled end.

"Let's risk a torch," said Nixter.

In a few moments, the passage lit up. Merryn stopped singing and gazed around at the slimy green-brown surface surrounding them. She could see no exit but the way they had come. She followed Nixter's eyes to the ceiling.

"See this surface above our heads? It's considerably smoother in texture than the surrounding wall. I am sure it's a doorway of some description, but I can't see any way of releasing it."

Suddenly, a grotesque face surfaced in front of Merryn. She'd stopped singing and the loireag looked murderous.

"Again ... again!"

"Don't," ordered Nixter abruptly.

The loireag leapt up at him clamping down on her nasty razor-edged teeth. Using the rope as a buffer, Nixter held her at bay. She lashed out repeatedly at the rope but he held it taut.

"Tell us how to get past and you can have a tune."

"Mistress says to keep stum."

"Ah, the entrance is hexed," murmured Nixter. "We need a counter-hex."

"Your mistress won't know," he soothed in a surprisingly oily voice. "We only want a peek and then your bird will sing. The mistress doesn't sing so prettily to you. She leaves you to hear those harsh sounds from above. We shall give you a pretty song, but we need to look first."

The loireag writhed and snarled, biting and lashing out at the rope.

"Just the words and she'll sing," oiled Nixter.

"Dead fisherman, dead fisherman, TOOOOOOOON!" she screeched at the end of her patience. She snatched the rope from Nixter's hand. Just as she was about to connect with his throat, Merryn let loose a soaring note. The creature's rage melted away and she slipped down and away from them. Merryn spotted Rohan, who had braced himself against the side of the wall ready to tackle the loireag from behind. He breathed deeply.

"Don't get too comfortable," said Nixter. "We've yet to see what's behind this door. First we have to work out the counter-hex. A dead fisherman! What could it mean? Do we know any?"

There was a long pause.

"Uncle Eddie was a fisherman," said Merryn.

"Who's Uncle Eddie?"

"Edward Moore, Auntie's husband. He died last year. His fishing boat capsized."

Nixter nodded slowly. "Lorelei's wedding band, I remember now. It appeared shortly after she first began to visit. I wonder … Stay back and remember what I said before we set out."

In a clear steady voice he spoke the name of Merryn's late great-uncle. The rock ceiling slid open in one steady motion.

What's Uncle Eddie got to do with this? Merryn removed her cap and folded it inside her pocket. Rohan, fur tucked inside his attached pack, checked the straps to make sure it was secure. Slowly, the three hoisted themselves up and peered inside.

Nixter's instincts had been correct. Above them was a large air-filled chamber. At the far end, lay three large bags. One was clearly marked *decorations*, another *gifts* and the third, *works*. Alongside the bags, in puddles of water, lay two coils of rope. Apart from these items, the chamber was empty.

"Quickly," commanded Nixter. "We'll take a bag each."

They clambered up into the chamber and made their way quickly across the dirt floor. They were a little more than half way there when Merryn cried out sharply.

"Stop! Don't move! Something's wrong. The floor — it's been planted with mines!"

Nixter stopped abruptly. "What do you mean? How do you know?"

"I've planted enough paintball mines in my time to know. Look down, at the floor. See those flat brown stones, the small ones that blend so well with the ground? Notice how they're randomly distributed, but there are none near the edges of the chamber. I'll eat my red cap if there aren't explosive devices below those marker stones. Rohan and I are okay, we haven't stepped on one, but Nixter …"

Nixter lowered his head and swallowed loudly. Just visible, beyond the contour of his elegant bare foot, was a flat brown stone.

Merryn spoke calmly. "You must stay as still as you can. We'll transfer something of equal weight to you or heavier, onto the stone. Then you must step away, slowly. It'll mean sacrificing a bag but better that than you."

"Use the bubbleworks," whispered Nixter. "If I'm going to blow, we might as well make it look decent!"

Merryn and Rohan made their way cautiously to the back of the cave. They took a bag each and dragged them slowly to the exit, taking great care to avoid the markers, before heading back for the bag of bubbleworks. They grasped it between them and working their way carefully across the floor, they arrived at Nixter's side. Although freezing inside the cave, beads of perspiration rolled down his face, dripping off the edge of his jaw. Together, Merryn and Rohan hoisted the heavy bag and placed it slowly down, taking care to cover the tops of Nixter's feet.

"Slowly, don't shuffle; just smoothly draw out one foot at a time. Place them well outside the stone," said Merryn.

Nixter wasn't listening. He was staring towards the end of the chamber, a sickened expression on his face. Merryn looked up. She followed the direction of his gaze.

"RUN!" he yelled.

They said goodbye to Rushida

An Urgent Plea

"O, train me not, sweet mermaid, with thy note

To drown me in thy sister's flow of tears…"

— William Shakespeare, *A Comedy of Errors*

Unravelling and coming towards them at great speed, were the two large coils of wet rope … only they weren't coils of rope. *How could they be?* Their bodies were thick and snake-like, scales gleaming. Tongues flicked menacingly between dripping fangs, the droplets burning holes in the cave floor. The writhing lengths of green and violet were serpents, or melusines to be correct. They must have been dozing when the three had first entered the chamber. If only they had looked more carefully.

Merryn and Rohan leapt for the exit as Nixter stepped out from under the bag and sped towards them. They flung themselves through the hole just as the bubbleworks toppled from their position in weighting the landmine.

"Edward Moore," shouted Nixter. The ceiling door closed as an explosive charge ripped across the floor above. They were thrown hard against the sides of the passage.

"SWIM!" cried Nixter.

Merryn forgot all about saving Winter Tide and focused on making her way to the blowhole. With tremendous effort, she reached the end of the passageway and entered the main tunnel.

"We're nearly there, swim faster," urged Nixter.

"They're coming," shouted Merryn. She'd paused to glance behind.

In the distance she could hear the water begin to draw. A powerful current sucked her backwards. Nixter's torch lit up the passage. To her horror, she saw a massive bubble, the circumference of the tunnel, speeding towards them. Two dangerously beautiful women reclined inside it.

"SWIM!" cried Nixter.

Heart pounding, Merryn tore through the water. She reached the blowhole just as the base of the bubble made contact and exploded with tremendous force. She was propelled forward and up. Before she could draw breath and brace herself, she lay stretched out and dazed on the area of bank surrounding the hole. Two ugly scaled heads, poised and ready to strike, burst upward. She screwed her eyes shut preparing for the worst, but then there was only silence. She opened her eyes, or at least half an eye. Nixter and Rohan lay in a tangled heap next to her. She opened her eyes fully and nudged them.

Nixter and Rohan rolled apart, chests heaving. Standing at the rim of the blowhole were the two beauties they had glimpsed inside the giant bubble. One was dressed in a glittering emerald gown, the other in violet. Long dark hair coiled around exquisite faces. Only the eyes revealed their true natures. At the centre of each chocolate brown iris lay a tiny gleam of orange. The melusines smiled at them in a slightly coy way before leaping back into the hole.

"They can't hurt us up here," panted Nixter. He clutched his cap and snatched deep breaths of fresh air. "Are you harmed?"

Merryn and Rohan checked themselves over and shook their heads.

"I'm sorry we couldn't rescue the festival," puffed Merryn, still struggling to catch her breath.

"We did our best," panted Nixter. "And at least we know where that tunnel leads to. Although the chamber we entered is probably one of many. But we must head back now. It's late and I've kept you from your beds long enough. I must report to Conang. He'll be waiting. To think I nearly didn't let you come. I placed you both in terrible danger. I hope you'll forgive me but the truth is I never would have made it back without your help."

The three hugged tightly before departing for their homes.

Merryn glanced behind her as she crept quietly towards her

house. In the distance she could see Rohan's figure disappearing along the path. Nixter's silhouette remained motionless by the blowhole waiting and watching. She looked forward. Her house was dark and all was quiet.

She was just creeping up the path to her back door when she noticed something. By the side of the path, reflected in the moonlight were small oblong puddles of water. They led from the paddock up to the patch of grass below her bedroom window. She made her way to them and crouched low. The puddles were footprints. Judging from the size of them, adult footprints. Their craters were filled with water. Strange, it hadn't been raining. Merryn suddenly felt very cold. An icy wind blew over her and she shivered. Without thinking, she dipped a finger into a puddle and sucked it. *Salt water*. She looked to the horizon for Nixter, only he'd gone. She rushed for the back door and turned the handle. Relief filled her. The door was unlocked. She stole inside quietly closing it and locking it behind.

She was halfway up the stairs when she froze. Staring down at the carpet she bit deeply into the side of her cheek. Beneath her feet, the carpet was wet. She followed the damp trail up the staircase … to her bedroom. Heart thudding, she approached the door and gently nudged it open. In the moonlight she could see her window was wide open, the curtains blowing outward. Her bed covers lay in a mess on the floor. The wardrobe doors were open and the box that housed Auntie's hat lay open on the floor. She slid open a dresser drawer. Its contents were strewn about. Slipping into her pyjamas, she walked to the wardrobe and closed it. She shut the bedroom window and locked it before rearranging the bed clothes. Climbing into bed, she pulled the covers tightly around her. *She knows where to find me.* Merryn lay in bed forcing herself to breathe. It was a long time before she fell asleep.

"Lucky your parents didn't wake," said Rohan, leaning against the canteen wall. "Even luckier you weren't there. I think we should tell Nixter straight away, like today, after school. It's the last week of term, nearly Christmas. Dad won't mind if I'm out a bit later than normal. I'll have to drop home for my rucksack first. I'll let him know I'm meeting you."

The bell sounded for the final class of the day and Merryn picked up her bag and followed Rohan out.

"I've got the cap with me. I was worried about leaving it in my room. I hope it's safe to go to Nixter's but I can't spend another night locked and bolted in my room. Mum tried to come in and check on me last night and nearly broke the door down when she couldn't open it. I told her I needed some privacy and now she's worried I'm turning into a teenager already. Nixter will know what to do. I'll meet you at the bay after school, as soon as you can get there."

They joined the throng of students making their way to class. Inside the main school corridor, they passed Huff and Berk. For the first time since the minefield incident, Merryn caught them looking at her. She made eye contact briefly then watched as they nudged each other and an evil glint was exchanged. *What's that about?* Deciding she had more important things to think about, she put them out of mind.

Arriving home, Merryn threw her school bag down and grabbed a couple of reindeer-shaped biscuits from a tray in the kitchen.

"Mum, I'm meeting my friend … err Rohan … at the beach. Be back later."

"Before dark and in time for dinner please. Why don't you invite him here sometime? We'd love to meet him. Promise not to embarrass you … can't vouch for your dad though."

"Err, sure Mum, maybe another time. Mum, can I ask you a quick question? It's about Aunt Lorelei. How did she and Uncle Eddie meet?"

Mum smiled and put down the biscuit cutter.

"Well, it was before my time but your grandmother, Auntie's sister, always called Lorelei *Eddie's Buoy* — spelt b u o y. It was a bit of a joke between them. Apparently, Auntie saved Edward's life. His boat capsized in Ben-Varrey Bay, he nearly drowned. Auntie rescued him … pulled him from the sea apparently. They were inseparable after that. What makes you ask?"

"Just curious. Thanks Mum. I'll see you later." Merryn grabbed another biscuit and headed for the back door.

She arrived at the bay the same time as Rohan and together they tore down the well-worn cobblestones and flung themselves onto the sandy beach. As she secured her cap, something moved suddenly from behind. She spun around but too late. In their haste, they'd forgotten to check for company. Before she could cry out they were tackled and locked into half-nelson holds from behind.

"Goin' fer a swim?" taunted Berk. His stiff red-blonde hair stood upright in the wind.

"In December! Freaks! Spose yer've got duck's feet too," spat Huff nastily. "We know yer pal 'ere has."

"No, I've got something much better!" Merryn concentrated and channelled energy downward. In moments, she had morphed an impressive tail.

In the second it took the pair to register and leap backwards in shock, Merryn and Rohan were in the water. Now they could only be seen from the waist up. Huff and Berk looked dumbstruck. Neither mentioned they'd just seen a girl with a fish's tail.

"Lovely day for a dip," teased Merryn.

"Like bath water," added Rohan.

They ducked below.

"Do you think that was a good idea?" asked Rohan as he swam downward.

"Better than losing my cap and your fur to them. Who are they going to tell? Kids with a fish's tails and webbed feet — swimming in December! No one would believe them."

They arrived at the entrance to Nixter's home and, as Rohan knocked, they heard an urgent "enter". It sounded almost like a plea. They glanced at each other before swimming hurriedly into the front room.

Nixter had company. Seated next to him was a lovely merrow. Dark hair rippled down over her hunched shoulders to her waist. Her huge dark eyes brimmed with tears. Nixter looked relieved to see them.

"This is Rushida Kumer. I'm afraid something rather serious has happened. Conang is on his way now to inform Lir. Rushida has been confronted by … the sea wraith. Although her story began some time ago, around the same time our cod were receiving their *vision*." Rushida shuddered and Nixter patted her back. The merrow stopped crying and held up a hand.

"I shall tell them Nixter my dear, though I'm thoroughly ashamed of my part. I lied, you see. I knew I was doing wrong but I was desperate." The wet eyes gazed forlornly at them. "Mr Kumer and I have been searching for a pearl for centuries. I'd not long returned from the South Sea, a journey of many leagues. I'd been away for the best part of a year and vowed it would be the last expedition of that kind. It was a sad decision and a strange time for me. It was during this time, on the rocks at Ben-Varrey Bay, that a seemingly kind old merrow approached me. She offered me the world — a pearl — my heart's desire! She just held out her hand and there it was. The one thing I'd spent most of my young life searching for. She said she'd come across it too late for herself and had no daughter to pass it on to. She could see my pain at not having a family of my own and urged me to take it.

"I couldn't believe my luck, after all that time. But with the offer came a condition. At some time, in the near future, she wished to borrow the shell containing the baby, but just for twenty-four hours. It seemed an odd request. However, she explained, that as she was too old to have a child of her own, she could experience a little of motherhood by spending time with the shell, as all mer-mothers do.

"Something felt terribly wrong at that point. It was her haste and insistence on sealing the bargain, all the while urging me to take the pearl. In the end, the desire for a family of my own was too strong. I agreed to her condition, took the pearl and put her out of my mind. Then came the lie. I told my husband and family I'd found the pearl by chance. The celebrations we had …

"I forgot about the promise until this morning — she knocked on my door. This time there was no kindness, no attempt at disguise. Aurelia Aquabelle is my friend, I knew who she was. She informed me she was taking the shell as agreed and would return it in twenty-four hours. Then she vanished completely.

"I thought the shell would be safe. The new Merling House deep under the courtyard of the palace is one of the most secure places in Turrey. I raced over and alerted Aquilis to the situation but it was too late. My shell had vanished. Every square inch of the room and nearby vaults was searched and double-searched, but there was no sign of it. Aquilis contacted Captain Conang, and I had to tell my husband the truth. He's a kind merman and forgave me, but he's desperately worried. He departed with the Captain to inform Lir. Then I remembered seeing your advertisement in the *Turrey Tribune*. I came at once. How could the shell disappear?"

Rushida put her head in her hands and began to weep again. Nixter placed his hand on her arm.

"Rushida, we still have time. But, in answer to your last question, there is no stronger magic in the world of water than the seal of a promise. It is sacred. Once you struck the bargain, the sea wraith could easily summon the shell. Her powers have grown such that she did not need to come in person to take it. Your shell went to her. The process, a remarkable thing, was instant. No guards or intervention could have stopped it."

"Nixter, what did you mean when you said we have time?" asked Merryn.

"I was about to explain. The shell is some hours from reaching what merrow refer to as *the quickening*. This is a precise time calculated soon after the pearl is placed inside the clam and it is sealed. It's the time when the weaving of the red cap is complete and its zenith of power peaks. If the cap were to be removed before this hour, it would be too weak to survive. In all probability it would just crumble away to nothing in the seawater. Once the binding is complete however, in theory, the cap could be removed and accommodate any wearer. The wraith is desperate to own a cap and return to the sea, but will not be stupid enough to open the shell before it has quickened. She will have it safely under guard, biding her time."

"What are we waiting for?" exclaimed Merryn.

"Quite right," said Nixter, leaping to his feet. "But this could be our most dangerous mission. I was nearly foolish enough to leave you behind once and would never have returned without your assistance."

"I think we should stay together," said Rohan. He looked at Merryn. "If you're up for it. You have the most to lose." He glanced up at her cap. "If you want to sit this one out ..."

Merryn pulled herself up. "Do I look like I want to sit it out?"

Rushida threw her arms around Merryn, then Rohan, causing him to turn the same colour as the cap.

She released them and Merryn and Rohan began to prepare for an expedition immediately, helping Nixter gather together necessary equipment.

"How will we know where to look?" asked Rohan.

"We can only try the most logical places first. We know that the most likely lair is a network of underground caves, below the cliff path. The shell must remain in seawater but the wraith cannot. She'll have it submerged but close to her ... and heavily guarded. Caves are the most likely place as they provide both of these conditions. We *have* to find another entrance."

There was silence as they busied themselves.

"I may know of one," announced Merryn suddenly.

Nixter looked up sharply. "Speak up," he urged.

She hesitated.

"Well ... I know someone who might be able to help ... at least ... I could ask."

"Is it someone we know?"

Merryn nodded. "Her name's Morag."

Nixter and Rohan looked back at her blankly.

"She's, err, a loireag."

"You're on first-name terms with a loireag ... the loireag?" Nixter looked incredulous.

Red-faced, Merryn nodded again. "It happened, yesterday evening, after one of Dad's, um, singing sessions. I could hear wailing coming from the cliff's edge. The whole family noticed it. Mum said it was probably a nesting gull or wind whistling through the blowhole. But I knew what it was. It went on and on. After a while it sounded a bit sad. I thought about how awful it is to have a sensitive ear and be forced to listen to Dad on a regular basis. I should know. I'm used to it now but it still grates. Then I thought how lucky I was to have a thing to listen to music with. I can slip on headphones and hear nothing else, just the sounds I love. That's when I first thought I could put her out of her misery — by lending her my player. It has some great music on it, stuff I thought she'd like.

"I sneaked out of the house after dinner and followed the sound to the cliff. I looked down and saw her. She was sitting in a pool of water on a ledge, outside an opening in the cliff. She howled when she saw me. I sang to her for a bit until she calmed down. Then I lowered the player and she took it. She didn't know what it was for at first. I had to mime to show her how it worked. When she figured it out and heard the first song, it was like I'd handed her heaven. It's hard to imagine but she actually tried to smile."

Rohan and Nixter looked at each other and shuddered.

"When were you thinking of telling us?" asked Rohan eventually.

"I ... I wanted to but I was a bit embarrassed. I wasn't sure if I what I'd done was okay. She's probably working for the sea wraith."

"It's never wrong to be kind to a fellow creature," said Nixter. "And in this case, your act of kindness may bring about some good. I think we should pay Morag a visit straightaway."

"Nixter, there's something else. The wraith — she came to my house — into my room — while we were in the tunnel the other night. My things had been gone through."

Nixter's face hardened. "She must not be allowed to get a cap."

"But how can we stop her? She won't give up will she?"

"We must find her and ... finish her." He whispered the last two words.

"You mean ... as in ...?"

"She showed Edward and Lorelei Moore no mercy and don't be fooled into believing she will show you mercy when she gets her cap back. She's gone too far to a darker side to be saved now."

"You mean Uncle Eddie ..."

Nixter snorted. "It was no boating accident last year. It was the beginning. Your aunt knew or guessed. I'm sure of it."

Merryn felt her fingers curl into solid fists. "Uncle Eddie

had another boat accident, a long time ago. That's how he and Auntie met. She saved his life." *Eddie's Buoy.*

Nixter looked at her, his eye's wide. "The final piece of the puzzle," he whispered. "She ... Murgen ... came back to finish what she started."

Before Merryn could ask Nixter to explain, he slung his bag across his shoulders abruptly.

"Follow me," he commanded.

They said goodbye to Rushida and one by one, she hurriedly kissed them.

"I'll remain. Conang and Lir will come soon," she said.

"We've no time to wait," said Nixter.

Lair of the Sea Wraith

"Deep in the bottome of the sea her bowre
Is built of hollow billows, heaped hye."

— Edward Spenser, *The Faerie Queene*

The three surfaced a few yards from the shore of Ben-Varrey Bay. Nixter pulled them down again.

"That was close. There's a policeman up there scanning the water. I don't think he saw us, but it was a near thing. We'll have to wait until he goes, or find another way to access the cliff. I doubt he'll be able to see me, but he will see you as clearly as he sees all other humans."

"Oops," said Merryn. She told Nixter what had transpired with Huff and Berk, earlier at the bay. "I didn't think they'd tell the authorities."

"You're full of surprises today!" Nixter exclaimed.
"Hopefully they won't be believed. Your policeman is just
making sure. Let's swim down and alongside the cliff."

Merryn swam to the front as they began to descend and
directed them to the area that was Morag's new home. Then
cautiously, they swam again to the surface. Nixter went first.

"He's gone. Let's climb."

The cliff was steep, but there were plenty of crags to ensure
a good foothold. Merryn's took the lead and soon pulled up
and over a ledge to find herself face to face with Morag.

The loireag glared horribly when she saw Nixter's head
appear. Merryn frowned at her. Like a sulking child, she pulled
headphones on and closed her eyes, submerging into a rock-
pool of seawater. She popped up momentarily to remind
Merryn not to forget the new memory card she'd been
promised.

"*Toons*, muckle *toons!*"

Behind Morag was the opening to a cave. They made their
way cautiously forward and were about to duck under the rim
to enter when the entire cave and ledge trembled violently, as
though an earthquake was reaching its apex. They heard a huge
roar then reeled as a hideous stench wafted over them.

Merryn glanced at Nixter. Terror showed clearly in his eyes.

"Trow breath. Quickly, against the ledge."

They pressed themselves against a ledge by the side of the
cave and ducked down low. Merryn could see clearly into the
cave now. She wished she couldn't. Lurching towards them,
bent double under the ceiling, was a creature of monstrous

proportions. Its skin was bluish grey in colour and its small eyes looked hard, as though they'd seen many wicked things. It had a great hairy hunch of a back and long, hairy muscular arms, one of which wielded a big club.

"Don't panic," said Nixter. "It won't … can't come out … not yet."

"W … what's a t … trow?" asked Rohan.

"I don't want to freak you but a sea-trow is a distant relative of the troll. I'm guessing you've heard of those? If anything, the trow is the more cantankerous of the two."

Merryn swallowed loudly. "What do you mean by *not just yet?*"

"Trows hate sunlight. They'll only visit the upper air after sunset. Trows who find themselves outside before sunset cannot return to their homes until darkness descends. This is the natural law that governs the trow. If we're fortunate enough to lure it outside, we'll have at least an hour to locate the shell and exit the cave before it can return."

"Lure!" exclaimed Merryn. "We're going to lure it out? Are you crazy?"

"We've no choice," replied Nixter. "Unless we start looking for another way in. That could take weeks."

"But how will we do it?"

"That all depends on how hungry it is." Nixter looked side-on at Rohan. "If it hasn't eaten for a while, it might be tempted by a tasty morsel of its favourite food."

"A … and what would that be?" stammered Rohan.

"That would be seal flippers."

"You don't mean … I'm not sure I … it won't eat me, will it?"

"Of course not," Nixter reassured. "The idea is to tempt it outside. Trows are slow-witted. Once it's realised it's out of the cave before sunset and can't return, seal flippers will be the last things on its mind. We'll be able to slip past and into the cave. But we must hurry, the sun is low."

Rohan took a deep breath and tugged his seal fur all the way up and over his shoulders, pulling the hood firmly over his head. For the first time, in front of them, he fully transformed. He was no longer a boy and strange as it seemed to Merryn, the transformation was beautiful. Rohan's sleek grey and silver coat gleamed in the soft light of dusk. Merryn shivered.

Taking her eyes from him momentarily, she pressed herself further against the ledge alongside Nixter, and waited. The rest would be up to Rohan.

She watched as he made his way to the opening and barked in a seal-like way. The result was terrifying.

The ledge rocked violently as the club swung down skimming the outside edge of the cave. Rohan dodged backwards as the great stick brushed past, barely missing him. Rock and shale showered around. Merryn felt the knot of fear tighten in her stomach. Being a seal out of water had made Rohan slow and clumsy. However, the trow looked equally slow. It took a step forward in compensation for Rohan's movement backward, then it blinked stupidly as the waning daylight hit its eyes. It didn't seem to register that it was close to exiting the cave. Dollops of green drool dripped down the sides of its mouth. Its primary focus was the seal. The trow was hungry.

Rohan began to clap in a teasing way. The trow lurched forward, its club lifted high. Down it came with a terrifying thwack! Merryn braced herself as another shower of rock-fall rained over them.

She bit down on her lip to stop herself from crying out as she saw how close the club had come again to her friend. Against her will she looked on as Rohan edged further back, the trow following. It hardly seemed to notice that it had stooped down low, to duck under the outer edge of the cave's mouth. The trow was outside in daylight. It let loose a great howl as Merryn, clutching Nixter's sleeve, dived into the cave. She spun around.

Rohan was moving towards them, but slowly. He managed to waddle halfway into the cave's entrance when something powerful locked around his tail. It was a massive fist. The trow wanted its seal, daylight or not. Merryn watched helplessly as the enormous creature lifted Rohan up. He looked so tiny in the great hand, like a tadpole held by a child. She knew he didn't have much time until the club came back down. Suddenly, Rohan threw his head back. He managed to flip the hooded section of his fur away allowing his human face to emerge. She cheered inside as he rippled along the length of his body, the fur dropping to his waist, freeing his hands.

The trow looked down. Surprised at the disappearance of

the tasty flippers, it dropped its catch into the pool of water containing the loireag. Rohan landed next to Morag with a great splash. He actually looked pleased to see her. She didn't look quite as happy to see him, and her mouth twisted into a nasty snarl. Tearing off his sealskin and clutching it, he leapt upwards and out of the water, and ran as fast as he could to the cave. The trow blundered forward. Rohan moved like lightning and was inside before the hairy arms could enfold him.

The trow thrashed at the cave's entrance but couldn't penetrate the opening. It was as though an invisible veil of the strongest cling film was stretched across it.

Merryn hugged Rohan tightly, then stepped back giving him a few moments to recover. Nixter reminded them that time was running out and they must push on.

"We must try to follow the cave system downward, if possible. The shell will be somewhere below water level."

They walked to the back of the cave and glanced about. It was dark and the cave's interior was icy cold and smelt horribly like old bins and sweaty feet. Nixter pulled out a torch and switched it on. The beam of light flashed across a rocky floor illuminating what must have been leftovers from the trow's last few meals. Merryn saw Rohan shudder as the light bounced off several mounds of discarded seal bones.

"We should split up and search the confines of the cave thoroughly," urged Nixter. "Unless they have been placed here as a decoy of some sort, the wraith would not waste a perfectly good loireag and sea trow on an empty cave. There must be a way out or down."

Merryn walked to the far right of the cave and lowered her head. She could hear a faint gurgling sound.

"I can hear something, over here. Listen."

Rohan and Nixter joined her at the back of the cave and lowered their heads.

"That sounds like water," said Nixter. "It's coming from below the cave floor."

They knelt down and placed their ears to the ground. Merryn could hear the sound clearly now. She was crouched next to a large rock.

"Let's shift this," she suggested.

All three pushed hard and the heavy stone moved aside. Below where it had sat was the beginning of a narrow passageway.

"Slippery starfish! This is more like it!" exclaimed Nixter. "If I'm not mistaken, this tunnel leads underwater. Although it looks awfully narrow. You two should manage it all right, but I'm not sure I shall fit. I think I could just squeeze through the opening, but if it narrows on the way down, I could get stuck."

"I'll go first," volunteered Rohan. "I'll try to let you know what's down there."

"Come straight back or let us know if it is safe to follow."

They watched as Rohan shoved the fur into his rucksack and held on to it tightly with one hand. He slipped easily into the slender opening and began to wriggle downward. As the passage curved, he disappeared quickly out of sight. Merryn

heard a great whooshing sound followed by a splash, then
silence. Nixter called down but there was no reply.

"It sounds as though he may be underwater, in which case
he'll not hear us until we are also submerged. I hope I'm doing
the right thing in going next. We can't leave Rohan down there
alone. I'll try to let you know if it's safe to follow."

Nixter pulled on his cap, morphed a long slippery tail and
climbed into the entrance. After a few seconds Merryn heard
him speak.

"It doesn't seem to ..."

The sentence trailed off and was followed by whooshing
and splashing, then silence. Merryn slapped on her cap and
climbed into the passage as quickly as she could. She wriggled
past a curve in the tight opening when suddenly, the walls
became silky smooth and she sped along what felt like tight
watery tube. She descended with a splash into a deep
underwater chamber.

Instantly, something wrapped tightly around her body and
with tremendous strength, moved her sharply away from the
passage opening. The chamber was darker than the inside of
the cave had been, and her eyes were slow in adjusting. With
relief, she felt the pressure around her body relax. She could
just make out the figures of Nixter and Rohan floating
alongside. Then she felt a sharp quiver of excitement. As her
eyes adjusted in the darkness, she could see the outline of a
giant clamshell. She felt Nixter's elbow in her side. Her eyes
went upwards. The quiver ebbed away. Guarding the shell was
the owner of the grabber that had moved her away from the

entry point, although grabber wasn't the right word. It had been a tentacle, but no ordinary tentacle. This one belonged to a giant octopus. Its huge body filled the chamber.

"Is that what I think it is?" she whispered.

"Yes … rare … normally docile … except expectant mothers … like this one."

"Err … Nixter?" interrupted Rohan. "What are we going to do next?"

"The wraith's taken her eggs … for bargaining power. We must find them."

Merryn watched as Nixter scanned the confines of the chamber. His eyes stopped just to their left. He was looking at a large crevice in the wall. Slowly, he unzipped his bag and pulled out a periscope. Edging towards the opening so as not to alarm the octopus, he lengthened the body of the scope until it slipped around the corner of the rocky opening. He focused for a few moments, adjusting its position. Then he remained perfectly still, in a state of deep concentration. After a minute, ever so slowly, he withdrew and slipped back to their side.

"In there … guarded over … a water leaper."

Nixter held the periscope out and they took turns in focusing and looking. As Merryn took her turn she spotted a creature the size of a small car. It looked like a gigantic toad, only it had no front limbs. In their place were great bat-like wings. Its tail had not dropped off during the 'tadpole' stage and had developed into a long extension with a forked end. Surrounding it, strewn about on the chamber floor, were

several sheep skeletons. It was hovering over a large net bag …
filled with clusters of tiny eggs.

"Don't be frightened," said Nixter. "They don't eat people,
just sheep. But … they're noisy! They can make a horrible
sound — to frighten sheep from cliff's edges, into the sea. It
could wake the dead. She'll be here if she hears it. We need to
feed it."

Nixter fell silent. Minutes ticked by. The sun would soon be
setting and the shell would be quickening.

"Would it eat a roast lamb sandwich?" asked Rohan
suddenly. "Dad made me one, after school. I didn't eat it. It's
in my pack."

"Why didn't you say so? Quickly, where is it?"

Rohan pulled out two sandwiches from his rucksack and
removed the plastic wrap. Without Antisag, the bread began to
disintegrate. The big chunks of medium rare lamb, however,
held together.

"I'll distract it with food while one of you sneaks in and
takes the eggs. "I'll go," said Merryn. "I'm the smallest."

She waited a moment while Nixter extended his arm
through the crack in the wall and propelled a piece of lamb
strongly through the water of the adjoining chamber. Putting
the periscope in place, he watched. Merryn received an all-
clear sign and heart pounding, she squeezed through the
narrow crack.

She watched as meat skimmed through the water. The
leaper rushed to it, wolfing it down and immediately looking
about for more. Nixter threw another piece as far away from

the eggs as possible and the leaper leapt at it. As it scrounged for a third piece of meat, Merryn inched forward and grabbed the bag. She was on her way back when she froze. The leaper had spotted her. However, as long as the food kept coming, it seemed oblivious to the eggs leaving. She squeezed back through the crack and immediately a huge tentacle reached out and snatched the bag. Another patted her on the head and a third squeezed Nixter tightly. The octopus forgot all about the shell and they were free to approach.

Nixter threw the water leaper a little more meat. Merryn saw his look of concern. The meat was nearly gone and she knew what that meant. But first, they had a more immediate problem. The shell was enormous. There was no way they could take it back through the narrow passage. Whatever magic had brought it here, they did not possess.

"There's only one way to do this," said Nixter. "We must remove the baby from the shell. We cannot take the shell."

"But won't the cap be destroyed?" asked Merryn.

"No! Unlike the sea wraith, we don't want to remove the cap from the baby. Cold seawater will pose the greatest danger. It could cause the little one considerable shock as the inside of the clam is much warmer than the water of our chamber. The baby is still growing and many months from reaching full strength. However this is secondary. First, we have to get the baby out of the shell before we run out of lamb. Since none of us knows the passage, this will not be easy."

Nixter tore the last chunk of meat into tiny pieces, trying to eke it out.

"How will the wraith open the shell?" asked Merryn.

"Brute force, probably. She cares nothing for the well-being of the baby. I'm guessing she'll smash the shell. They can't be prised open. I don't know what to suggest."

"Do you know the passage your own mother used for your shell?"

"Why, yes! She used the initials of her favourite garden ornament, red coral. So like a Scandinavian merrow to be logical," mused Nixter. "The initials of the coral also matched the initials of her name, Raya Crystal."

"Where's Rushida from?"

"I think both she and her family hail from the Red Sea. I'm beginning to follow you. Now let me see, merrow from this region prize music and culture above all else; although food follows closely behind. Rushida Kumer, R.K, it's worth a try …"

"Red kale," began Merryn, blurting out the first thing that came to mind. "I think it's a type of cabbage."

"Ronan Keating, the Irish singer," said Rohan.

They paused staring at the shell. Seconds passed but nothing happened.

"Rudyard Kipling," suggested Nixter.

"Red ketchup," said Merryn. "Err, sorry."

"Ronald King," tried Nixter again. "The British artist. He's produced some quite spectacular embroideries of jellyfish …"

Silence followed as the three struggled to think of anything else that could possibly constitute a likely passage. Nixter frowned and stroked his beard as Merryn paced the chamber floor and Rohan twiddled with the straps of his rucksack. Vital minutes ticked away.

Finally Nixter spoke again. "I'm sorry but we can't afford to waste more time on this, although it was a commendable suggestion. We must force the shell. We risk harming the baby but we've no alternative."

"I know," shouted Rohan interrupting, "Rimsky Korsakov!"

Three pairs of eyes jumped back to the shell. They held their breath, but sadly, the lips of the clam remained tightly sealed. Then Merryn uttered the next logical phrase that entered her head.

"*Arabian Nights*."

The clamshell sprung open.

Nixter leapt upwards.

"JUMPING JELLYFISH! You've done it!" he cried. "I can't believe it! You've really done it. Marvellous assistants … and the words … they don't even bear Rushida's initials! What in the name of Neptune made you say them?"

"I don't know! Rohan and I once had a memorable English lesson to that piece of music. I must have somehow connected the word *Arabian* with Rushida's birthplace. Ooh, look!" she gasped, gazing into the shell.

Their focus turned to the clam and they were rendered silent. Nestled, deeply asleep inside its soft interior, was a tiny mer-baby. Her *cohuleen druith* sparkled and glittered, framing the wisps of silky golden hair that sprang beyond it.

A tiny silver tail curled around the base of the shell and, sleeping soundly in the space between, was a robin and a money spider.

"Look!" said Nixter. "The spider and robin have finished the cap and slightly ahead of time, too — it has quickened! They'll be exhausted. We must get them safely back to land. It would not bode well for us to leave them behind. They've done a wonderful job; she's a beauty!"

"She's gorgeous!" murmured Merryn.

Even the octopus took her gaze from her eggs for a moment to stroke the shell.

Suddenly, the three clapped their hands over their ears and jumped backwards as the most awful blood-frosting scream filled the chamber. The sound was hideous; like the scraping of chalk on a blackboard amplified over and over … and that couldn't begin to describe it.

"The water leaper," said Nixter, after the noise had finally ceased and they had removed their hands from their ears. "The lamb ran out some minutes ago. We haven't long. But … we have another problem. Once we remove the baby from the shell, she may perish in the cold."

"I've been thinking about that," said Rohan. "Would my fur help?"

Merryn felt a jolt of panic. Just as she opened her mouth to protest, Rohan pointed to the roof of the cave, many feet above them. She saw at once that towards the left-hand edge of the air-filled upper chamber was a tiny shaft of daylight.

"The truth is we need your fur desperately," said Nixter. "If

I wrap her in the fur of a selkie, she will be as safe and warm as if in her own shell. We can transfer her to a new shell once we reach Turrey."

Nixter pulled from his kit a long length of knotted rope attached to a metal hook. Like an expert, he cast the hook high into the air until it caught on an area of rock ledge just near the shaft of light. Next, he passed Rohan a small metal pickaxe, to assist him in breaking through to the outside.

Carefully, Rohan picked up the sleeping bird and spider and placed them gently inside his shirt pocket, covering this with his seal skin. Grabbing the end of the rope, he hoisted himself up and climbed quickly and nimbly. He reached the air in no time and removed the fur, casting it below.

A great rumbling filled the chamber. The floor and walls around them shook.

"She's coming," announced Nixter.

Merryn marvelled at his calm. She trembled violently, fumbling for her cap to make sure it was secure. Nixter grabbed Rohan's discarded fur and lifting the mer-baby from her bed, he wrapped it delicately around her tiny body. Cradling her, he made sure she was well covered. Motioning for Merryn to follow, he made swiftly for the passage they had entered through.

Suddenly, there sounded an almighty crack. They were moments too late. In front of the entrance they sought, stood a terrifying spectre.

Struggling against the waves of fear that had turned her to jelly, she took strength from Nixter and mustered the courage to look up. Hovering less than a foot away was a ghastly hag of a creature that resembled neither merrow nor human. As the withered face came into focus, the first thing Merryn noticed about it was its nasty mouth. It was set like stone in a down-turned, sour expression that those who have lived a mean and miserable life, often inherit. Merryn met the eyes next and watched them blaze with malicious intent as they fastened on the two intruders. Recognition registered and the expression changed from fury to a kind of mad, horrible pleasure. Her mouth opened to speak and, in stark contrast to the figure in front of them, a light musical sound emerged. It seemed that the one original aspect of the sea wraith that remained, was her pretty voice. But then, as she spoke, the words dripping in venom, the enchanting tones became quite easily, the scariest thing about her.

"Merryn O'Reilly! What a sweet pleasure, and so unexpected. You're the picture of your great-aunt. And what a beautiful headpiece you have. I used to have one just like it.

"Dr Havmand, it's been a long time. My, haven't you grown. Quite the handsome young merrow ... but alas, no manners to complement. A great pity. So very rude to drop in unannounced and take what isn't yours."

"Just taking back what isn't yours, in fact," Nixter replied briskly.

"Oh, but you're mistaken. It is mine. I made a bargain in good faith, to own this possession for some twenty-four hours. I don't believe my time has yet lapsed."

"Your time may not have lapsed but your good faith has. You

have no intention of treating this possession, as you call it, with the care and reverence it deserves. There is only one part you value and it isn't the tiny life of one of your own."

"And I used to think that you were one of the few amongst us with at least part of a brain that functioned. How soft and stupid you've become, just like the rest of them — turning to sponge over a baby, and a merrow one at that. Pah!" she spat nastily into his face. "What have merrow done for me? Did they help me get back my life, my future? They left me to suffer and live a half shell of an existence, banished, friendless and loveless. I turned my back on merrow a long time ago."

Nixter continued unperturbed. "You were a merrow once and you were raised under merrow law. Your cap was yours alone to protect. Once you come of age, you cannot place the burden of its care onto others. You put the mindless pursuit of a human first and took your eyes off your most precious asset. What happened was no one's fault but your own. Now, you want to make an innocent pay the price."

"Mindless," whispered the wraith. "Love is never mindless. Neither is hate for that matter … and I have hated for much longer than I ever loved. My hate is clever."

Her emerald claws rippled in the water and two serpent forms appeared either side.

"I won't bother to introduce my companions; I believe you have met. I shall make a bargain with you Dr Havmand. You can keep that precious baby intact in exchange for something else. You may leave, but your friend cannot. She has something far more valuable to me than the infant. Take it and go now, before I change my mind."

Nixter looked torn. He gazed at Merryn and then into the innocent face cradled in his arms, a tiny member of his own species. Merryn knew that the only reason he was being spared was the wraith's pleasure in seeing the pain of his choice. She knew which one he would make, and it was the one she wanted.

"Go!" cried Merryn. "What are you waiting for?"

The sea wraith flung her head back and laughed, sweet musical tones laced with malice. Then she spotted Rohan high above. He'd nearly reached the opening but must have paused, frozen, as the wraith issued her ultimatum.

She cast up her hand and directed a bolt of destructive energy upward but at that very second, the water turned black and the bolt missed its mark. The octopus had emptied herself of ink, helping in the only way she could. Nixter grabbed Merryn and tried to pull her to him and into the passage — but she was chained to the spot. In his heart, Nixter had made his choice and sealed another bargain. Merryn now belonged to the wraith.

"Go," she cried again, this time pushing Nixter and his precious bundle towards the passage.

He squeezed her arm and fled upward into the black as a great rumbling sounded from above. An avalanche of stones and rocks pelted down, the chamber of water breaking their fall. As the water cleared and the fall of rubble ceased, Merryn stood to face her alone.

...she loved the fisherman

The Memory Bubble

"They live their animated lives, and were
The sea to disappear, still would they live…
In the depths of a gently stirring imagination"
—— Susan Joslin, *You Have to Believe*

A clawed hand reached out to touch the red cap then pulled sharply back.

"It's been a long time," the sea wraith whispered. "But first I must deliver something in return. This is for Lorelei Moore, who denied me satisfaction to the end."

She spat out these last words before granting the melusines a silent signal. They writhed forward towering either side of Merryn, just as they had their mistress. As Merryn looked into the face of the sea wraith, the serpents reared their horrible heads and lunged forward, fangs dripping. She felt an indescribable sear of pain and pitched forward onto the chamber floor.

Moments before blacking out, she gazed up at the serpents. Strangely, in front of her, they disappeared into puffs of violet and green. The wraith appeared in their place. She looked murderous. Lifting the twisted index finger of her left hand and pointing it directly at Merryn, she mustered what seemed like all of her bitterness and bile, and channelled it downward, uttering a horrible curse. She flung this poisonous rage forth. Instinctively, Merryn twisted her head to one side as a nasty bolt of green light speared towards her. It stopped sharply, hovering momentarily in front of the small green shamrock attached to the side of the cap. At a vicious speed, it turned on itself and travelled back to its creator. The wraith uttered a tiny cry of surprise. With a loud crack, she vanished as quickly as her serpents. The last thing Merryn remembered was a tentacle wrapping around her middle and lifting her upward and into the passage through which she had entered.

Floating through velvety blackness, Merryn could see a small star of light. It came from above. *Rohan!* Had he managed to climb out of the chamber? She tried to pull herself up but a pair of strong hands held her down. *The wraith* … No, the wraith had gone. She'd seen it. Her eyelids felt heavy and they fluttered a few times before opening halfway. There was Rohan. *What's wrong with his head?* And Nixter, and Rushida, still crying. *The baby* … Merryn struggled to sit up, but again the hands pushed her down.

"Rest now. Don't try to move just yet."

"The baby! What happened?" Merryn cried out hoarsely, her neck and throat burning.

"The baby is fine," replied Nixter. "Thanks to you. She is on her way back to Turrey. Don't mind Rushida. This time they're tears of joy. Try to sit up and drink. Slowly now, you've survived the bites from two melusines. You've also lost blood. The drink will help to restore you."

With assistance, Merryn propped herself against a mound of pillows and sipped on the cup of hot sweet liquid Nixter pressed to her lips. Feeling suddenly stronger, she opened her eyes fully and saw that she was stretched out on the comfortable sofa in Nixter's front room. She turned slowly to Rohan and unable to help herself, grinned broadly.

"What happened to you?"

"Oh this?" He touched the side of his head. "Dad overdid it a bit with the bandage. Enough about me. Don't keep us hanging! What did you do to the sea wraith?"

Three eager faces looked down at her and Rushida momentarily stopped crying. Pausing only to sip the drink, Merryn told them what had transpired in the chamber.

After a long pause Nixter sighed deeply. "Instead of just taking the cap, easy enough, she wanted more. She wanted to hurt you terribly in the process. The resentment she must have held for Lorelei, was transferred to you. She didn't think logically. Your cap was originally woven for her and retains something of her spirit within it. She could never do harm to her own cap. What she didn't realise is that this property would also extend to a new owner. Any malicious moves towards her cap would be repelled back to their maker. With the melusines it proved fatal. They're very hard to kill; only the bite from another melusine will do it. They were acting for the wraith under her instruction. Their poison was repelled from 'her' cap back onto them. The same happened to the wraith. She inadvertently received a dose of whatever she intended for you.

"Do you remember what happened after you entered the passage?"

Merryn struggled to recall.

"I was there, with the baby," said Nixter. "A powerful hex barred the way. It was destroyed when the wraith fled. She wanted me to think I could escape only to pull me back to show what she had done to you. No doubt she intended to destroy us all. You were barely conscious but managed the journey back here — with a little help."

"The trow! How did we get past?"

"It was Morag who helped in the end. I think the sound of his moaning and whining to get back inside the cave must have got on her nerves. When we emerged from the cave they were sitting in the rock pool sharing her headphones, an earpiece each. They had no interest in us.

"When we arrived back here, Lir was waiting with a shell. He'd read his stargazing pond for guidance and rightly intuited that we might need one. We transferred the baby, who by the way, slept soundly throughout and I sent Conang back to Ben-

Varrey Bay with Rohan's fur. Rohan was there, head bandaged but desperate to see you. I'll let him tell you the rest."

"I was lucky to get here at all," said Rohan from his kitchen chair. "Dad would've had me grounded for a week.

"It's nothing, really," he added, touching the bandage. "I caught a rock on the side of the head as I was making my way out — too slow. When I saw her I froze. I wanted to help but didn't know what I could do. Then she saw me. Thanks to the octopus, she missed me, but the bolt she flung created a small avalanche. I'd just managed to shove the rucksack through the crack, and was trying to widen it to push myself through, when a rock dislodged. It hit me on the head and I fell onto a ledge below the opening. I think I'd still be there if Dad hadn't found me."

"Your dad found you!"

"Yeah, and by chance. Huff and Berk did go to the police. They told Quirk they'd seen us swim underwater without resurfacing. Luckily they left out the part about your tail. Quirk knows Huff and Berk but thought he'd better check out their story, just in case. He dropped by the house to see Dad. Dad guessed straightaway where we must be and managed to put him off. Told him I was inside doing homework if he'd like to take a look. Took a bit of a risk but Quirk just muttered something about what he thought of time-wasters, and left in a hurry.

"After he'd gone, Dad headed across to the bay, to see if he could find us. That's when he saw my rucksack, poking up through the soil. He dug down a bit and found me asleep on the ledge. I think the shock of seeing the wraith, followed by a bump on the nut, put me to sleep. I remember lying down and closing my eyes, then nothing 'til I heard Dad calling. He took me straight home. I had to beg him to let me come back and see if you'd made it out. I still can't believe I slept through the best bit!

"We should go soon though — if you're feeling better? Dad's waiting for us."

Suddenly a loud voice rumbled from behind.

"How's the dragon slayer?"

It was Conang with Lir and two mermen Merryn hadn't seen before. One rushed to Rushida's side.

"I think the Captain's asking if you're feeling better," laughed Lir. "I can't tell you how relieved we are that you all returned safely … and with the baby! It's nothing short of a miracle. Still, I can't help feel the teensiest bit sorry for Murgen Merryweather. She was a nice merrow once." He paused for a moment. "I think the Kumers have something for you Merryn."

Holding Rushida's hand, Mr Kumer stepped forward and handed her a small but beautifully wrapped package. His lower lip trembled.

Excited, Merryn ripped open the package. Inside was a piece of the most beautiful fabric she'd ever seen. It was exquisitely light and draped liquid-like into rainbow-coloured folds. It was a scarf, exactly what she needed to get past her family without an inquisition about the holes in her neck.

"I hope you like it?" said Mr Kumer. "It's fairy-made and has been in our family for generations. We want you to have it."

Rushida gripped his hand tightly. "Thanks to you, to all of you, we now have something far more precious to replace it with." She stepped forward and draped the scarf elegantly around Merryn's neck. It felt cool and light, and instantly soothed the area of burning around the bite marks.

The second merrow moved out of the shadows and swam forward. He had a long white beard and pink tinged his green cheeks. *He looks like a merrow Father Christmas*, thought Merryn.

"Hello, I'm Gilly, Gilly Greensleeves." The merrow reached deep inside his pocket and pulled out a spherical-shaped object. It was the size of a ping pong ball and like the scarf, shone in iridescent rainbow shades.

"This is for you … from Lorelei. It's a memory bubble. She came to see me, not long before she died." Gilly bowed his head briefly. "She was deeply troubled and wanted to place some information in a safe place. The bubble was her idea. It was an easy feat for me to perform. I have no idea of the content but she said I was to give it to Merryn, if and when I ever came across you. I first heard of you this morning when I was talking to Lir — about the theft of the festival works. I rushed straight home to get it. I hope I'm not too late." He reached over and placed the bubble in her hands.

Merryn held it as though it were the most fragile of eggs. Gilly laughed deeply and infectiously.

"It won't break. My bubbles are tough as shark skin."

"What do I do with it?"

"When you're ready, you need to pierce the skin. I suggest a nice hot bath and any old needle or pin will do the trick. It won't break until you're ready to hear."

"What will I hear?"

"Now that I don't know but only you will hear it. It's been nice meeting you. Good luck."

Merryn finished her drink and clutching her gifts and a jar of special ointment from Nixter, to help speed up the healing of her neck, she and Rohan said their goodbyes.

Made slow with fatigue, they swam back to Ben-Varrey Bay. Rohan's dad was on the beach, anxiously waiting for them. He looked relieved to see them and helped them from the water. They leaned against him as they made their way against soft apricot hues of twilight, towards home.

Rohan walked Merryn to her front door and as she stepped inside, he waved to her mother through the kitchen window.

"Nice scarf! Exquisite! Wherever did it come from?" gasped Mum.

"Um … just a present from a friend," stammered Merryn.

"Must be a pretty special friend," winked Mum. "Like the one with the nice dark eyes."

Merryn made a rush for the stairs. As she began to climb there was a sharp knock on the front door. Mum opened up to greet PC Quirk. Merryn waved down from the landing above and watched as the policeman snorted loudly.

"Sorry to waste your time girls," he said. "Had a report earlier about your youngest going missing at sea … from a couple of boys who are not far from the wrong side of the law."

"Why, Merryn's here!" exclaimed Mum, "and I can assure you she was dry as a bone when she came in."

"They needn't think they can get away with this one," muttered Quirk. "Wasting valuable police time and being a thorough nuisance. A little community service is in order. A few weeks of after school public pool cleaning and rubbish collecting, will make them think twice about sending me on a wild goose chase. Evening ladies."

Perfect, thought Merryn as Mum waved goodbye and closed the door.

"Just taking a bath Mum."

She dashed into her room briefly grabbing fresh jeans and a long sleeved t-shirt. Entering the hallway again, she stepped into the nearby bathroom and locked the door behind her. She turned the bath taps on and reached deep into the side pocket of her jeans pulling out the memory bubble. Water gushed into the tub. She held the bubble up to the light and watched for a moment as the rainbow shimmer revolved around its glassy surface. Tearing her eyes from the bubble, she dug deep into a bathroom drawer for a safety pin. She quickly undressed and climbed into the water, closing her eyes as the warmth washed over her.

Submerging her body up to her chin and taking a deep breath, she held the bubble to the light once more and plunged the pin into its side. It disappeared leaving a faint rainbow smear on the surface of the water. As the smear evaporated, a familiar presence filled her head and senses — the faint smell of the sea mixed with lavender. She blinked fighting back tears. Still clutching the pin she closed her eyes and listened as Aunt Lorelei whispered softly to her for the last time.

Hello Merryn. You can hear me. You have the Cohuleen Druith and know its purpose. I always intended for you to have it when the time was right but it has come to you early with no guide and burdened with trouble. This trouble is of my own making although I did not foresee it. This is a consequence of my nature. I have never dwelled in the past and live only for the moment. This is an honest account of how I came to have it.

I was some eight years older than you and found myself walking along the cliff path to Ben-Varrey Bay. From calmness came a sudden terrible storm. I took shelter on a ledge below the cliff. Looking down, I could see a small fishing boat, the fisherman fighting for his life. In the brief moment I watched, the oars were ripped from his hands and the boat tipped into the sea. As I climbed from the shelter to help I saw an oar cast onto the sand of the bay. I ran down the path and took it. Climbing out onto a rocky outcrop I held out the oar. Just as he reached it and I began to reel him in a merrow appeared. This will come as no surprise to you. By now you have seen them and know them to be as real as yourself. I had no such knowledge but what I did know from the blaze of fire in her eyes, was that she had been the cause of the tempest … and that she loved the fisherman.

"Mine," she shouted and tried to snatch the oar from my hands. I acted instinctively thinking only of saving the poor man. I grabbed a redcap from her head hoping to distract her for a moment. It did and I pulled the man to safety. We were away and up the cliff path before I

realised I still had the cap in my hands. But, the creature had just tried to kill a man, I gave no thought to returning it.

Time passed. The fisherman became Uncle Eddie and I discovered the purpose of the cap ... or it discovered me. It drew me to the sea like a magnet and I found a world I was more at home in than my own. By the time I knew of the consequences for Murgen, I guessed it to be too late for her. I have a practical nature and looked only forward.

It has been nearly a lifetime but my actions have finally caught up. The first inkling came recently when your great-uncle died. Despite his age he was a master sailor, as at home on the sea as myself. I knew his death to be no accident. Shortly after, I woke one night. A fierce storm blew outside and rattled at the windows. I got up to secure the latch and saw her face ... at my window. It was only for an instance and greatly altered but I knew it to be her and that she was back to claim what was once hers. I thought long and hard about returning the cap but in that brief moment at the window, I sensed inside her a deep wickedness. I love Turrey too much to risk unleashing it so I have passed the care of the cap to you. It will be a burden and may place you in mortal danger but it will also give you an incredible experience and the opportunity to form the deep friendships I sense you have not achieved on earth. I beg your forgiveness for making these assumptions. I have the deepest faith in you.

Goodbye my dearest and enjoy.

The lavender presence ebbed away. Merryn felt a sudden strong desire to be dry — to feel air on her skin instead of water. She splashed her face several times before climbing out of the tub. She dried hastily and threw her clothes on before making her way to her bedroom. Pulling the red cap out of her pocket, she placed it in its original box next to a framed photograph of Aunt Lorelei.

Goodbye Auntie ... and thank you! Merryn said the words in her head, a little like the way in which she spoke underwater. Suddenly, a ray of brilliant red light shot out from a tiny crack in the corner of the box. It came almost like a reply. She opened the box and removed the cap, this time holding it aloft. She stared at it for a moment but it seemed just as it had before — an ordinary looking swimming cap.

About the author:

Catherine Copeland is an Australian living on the Isle of Man. She was educated at New South Wales and Sydney Universities and is a secondary school teacher of Dance and History and a member of the Manx Ballet Company.

www.theunderwaterdetectives.com

About the artist:

Artist Marjolein Scott-van der Hek lives and produces her silk artwork on Abaco in the Bahamas. Her commissioned paintings can be found in private and corporate collections in America, Australia, Europe, the Far East and the Bahamas.

www.barefoot-contessa-art.com